The Duke That I Marry

By Cathy Maxwell

The Spinster Heiresses
THE DUKE THAT I MARRY
A MATCH MADE IN BED
IF EVER I SHOULD LOVE YOU

Marrying the Duke
A DATE AT THE ALTAR
THE FAIREST OF THEM ALL
THE MATCH OF THE CENTURY

The Brides of Wishmore
THE GROOM SAYS YES
THE BRIDE SAYS MAYBE
THE BRIDE SAYS NO

The Chattan Curse
THE DEVIL'S HEART
THE SCOTTISH WITCH
LYON'S BRIDE

THE SEDUCTION OF SCANDAL
HIS CHRISTMAS PLEASURE
THE MARRIAGE RING
THE EARL CLAIMS HIS WIFE
A SEDUCTION AT CHRISTMAS
IN THE HIGHLANDER'S BED
BEDDING THE HEIRESS
IN THE BED OF A DUKE
THE PRICE OF INDISCRETION
TEMPTATION OF A PROPER GOVERNESS
THE SEDUCTION OF AN ENGLISH LADY
ADVENTURES OF A SCOTTISH HEIRESS
THE LADY IS TEMPTED
THE WEDDING WAGER
THE MARRIAGE CONTRACT
A SCANDALOUS MARRIAGE
MARRIED IN HASTE
BECAUSE OF YOU
WHEN DREAMS COME TRUE
FALLING IN LOVE AGAIN
YOU AND NO OTHER
TREASURED VOWS
ALL THINGS BEAUTIFUL

CATHY MAXWELL

The Duke That I Marry

A SPINSTER HEIRESSES NOVEL

AVONBOOKS

An Imprint of HarperCollinsPublishers

First Avon Books mass market printing: December 2018
First Avon Books hardcover printing: November 2018

Print Edition ISBN: 978-0-06-286875-6
Digital Edition ISBN: 978-0-06-265579-0

FIRST EDITION

18 19 20 21 22 LSC 10 9 8 7 6 5 4 3 2 1

This one is for Kathryn Falk

The Duke
That I Marry

Chapter 1

Mayfield, the Country Estate of the Duke of Camberly
September 8, 1813

You are trying my patience, Matthew," the imperial voice said from his study door. "Have you forgotten you are to be in London for your wedding on the morrow?"

In the thin light of an overcast morning, Matthew Addison, recently named Duke of Camberly, looked up from the desk where he had been poring over ledgers to coldly eye his grandmother. Minerva, the Dowager Duchess of Camberly, was a handsome woman, over seventy in age, but she moved as if younger. Her hair was silver, and she wore her black with a touch of purple for her late husband and their oldest son and heir, William, whom she had adored with a passion. Both had passed within less than six months of the other a little over a year ago. She had not bothered to take off her coat, hat, or gloves. Instead, she had apparently arrived and come right for him.

Unfortunately, she had chosen the wrong moment to make an appearance. It was almost as if the suspicions in his mind had conjured her.

"Hello, Grandmother." He did not rise. "I have not forgotten. How can I? You've been sending me letters reminding me of my responsibilities every day for the past several weeks."

"*Because you are supposed to be in London,*" she snapped. "People are talking. There are wagers being made that you will not show. Leland Reverly is *not* pleased."

"London is only three hours away. I'll be there before the appointed time on the morrow. After all, everyone knows I need money. I really have no choice."

Matt was expected to wed Miss Willa Reverly, known as the Reverly Heiress and a woman he barely knew. He had nothing against Miss Reverly. She was like every other well-bred young miss with a rich father. Although if he remembered correctly—and his memory was a bit hazy—she was far more attractive than most.

That still didn't mean his upcoming marriage set well with him. He'd come to hate being the Duke of Camberly. The bloody, impoverished title had sucked *everything meaningful* out of his life.

Minerva frowned as if sensing something was not right between them. Her gaze took in the ledgers stacked and spread across his desk. She shut the door and approached him, taking the chair in front of his desk where she perched upright. "What is the matter with you?" she asked. "Why have you holed yourself up in here? I've heard reports that you have rarely strayed from this study."

"Oh, I've strayed, Grandmother. I've walked the estate from one end to the other."

She looked at him as if he'd said the most preposterous thing she'd ever heard. "Why would you do that?"

"Because I own it. Because I inherited a mess and I know nothing about land management and crops and breeding." And because, after the fool he'd made of himself in front of the *ton* over Letty Bainhurst, he'd thought to recover his self-respect by doing what was honorable and right. He had wanted to step up to the title.

Instead, he'd uncovered one mystery after another until, that very morning, he'd reached a terrible realization.

But his grandmother did not know this. She smiled. "Yes, however, you are going to marry Miss Reverly, and her dowry will set everything to rights." There it was: selling his name and person into marriage was merely a simple solution, and Matt rebelled. He became direct.

"What happened to the money, Grandmother?"

For the first time since she'd barged into the room, Minerva looked hesitant. "The money?"

Matt tapped the top ledger. "The money in the estate."

"You know what happened. Times have not been good for Mayfield. We discussed this after Henry died and we sat with George to go over matters." Henry was her late husband, the old duke. George was Matt's second cousin and a well-respected lawyer. "The estate was losing money. It just all went away."

"It did disappear," Matt agreed, his voice tense. "Money came in and yet was not spent on the estate at all. In fact, as little as five years ago, there had been plenty for repairs and improvements—and then it appears to have vanished. Decent tenants left because of unfulfilled promises over cottages with leaking roofs. The stables were emptied of good horseflesh, and the beasts in the fields from the pigs to the cattle, if they had any worth, were sold—except that money doesn't show where it went in the ledgers, either. Worse, I've learned that Grandfather stopped the servants' and workers' wages."

"Running the estate is expensive. I warned you—"

"Aye, you did. You said I would walk into Mayfield and see that everything of value had been sold off. All the books, the portraits, the furnishings are gone, except, according to these older ledgers, there should have been no need to sell them."

His grandmother laughed, the sound almost frivolous, convincing him more than anything else that she knew the truth. "What are ledgers?" she said. "You know Henry was not good with details."

"Actually, at one time, Grandfather had a competent manager, whom he abruptly let go before taking over managing the estate himself. And then it appears he willfully *bankrupted* it."

The dowager jumped on the force behind the word "bankrupted," the purple plume on her black bonnet shaking. "He tried his best."

Matt leaned back in the chair, dumbfounded. "His best? He didn't spend the money on seed or wages. Years ago there was plenty, and now it is gone. My grandfather was not a gambler and if he was into whores—"

"He would never touch one."

"Good, because for the amount of money I've found missing, there aren't that many whores in England."

Her chin came up. "I do not like your tone. Especially toward my late husband." She even added a dramatic quiver to her voice. "You don't understand the workings of an estate like Mayfield. You are a scholar and a poet—"

"Grandmother, what I am *not*, is a fool."

That snapped her mouth shut.

Matt leaned forward. "You know what happened to the money. You and Grandfather were as one. You even finished each other's sentences. Someone either robbed the money from the accounts or deliberately removed it, and what I want to know is why. To what purpose?"

"A good one," she answered, her voice faint.

"And that is?"

Instead of answering, her gaze hardened. She stared at some point in the far corner of the room, her black gloved hands clutched tightly in her lap.

Matt rose from the chair and came from behind his desk to her. He was a tall man, a good six foot five. "On the morrow, I'm marrying a woman I barely know to save Mayfield. One of my expectations in life was to marry for love."

"Like your father?" Minerva's tone was bitter.

"Yes, like him." Matthew's father had been Stephen, the second son, the one who had never followed the family's dictates.

"Wasting himself on an actress," she said with disgust.

"He married the woman he loved," Matt corrected. He had years of experience in deftly fending off his grandparents' barbs toward his mother. "And Father had no regrets, even when you and Grandfather disowned him for marrying her."

There was a beat of silence and then Minerva said, "She wasn't even that good of an actress."

"No, but she was a brilliant mother."

Minerva's pale eyes glanced at him as if to see if he jested. He didn't.

Matt had loved his parents very much. He'd been the youngest of five and the only son. The next oldest sibling to him was Amanda, and she was eight years his senior.

When his parents had been taken by fever, his sisters had brought ten-year-old Matt to their grandparents. His oldest sister, Alice, had told him it was the hardest thing she'd ever done, and yet, the four of them believed it was best for him.

The reception had been very cool. Alice had to set aside her pride to ask for help. In the end, her grandparents had given her what she'd wanted, an education for Matt and what she called, "his rightful place in Society."

Those years in private school had been lonely and hard. His grandparents and his uncle William had given him very little of their interest. His sisters had been there for him. However, they had their own struggles. Several married. The unmarried one, Kate, went into the theater as their mother had. Matt learned the difficult lesson that life could consume the best of intentions.

Fortunately, he had proven to be a stellar student, especially since his grandfather, the old duke, had made it clear Matt would be receiving no support from him. And then life changed.

Matt had been working as a tutor when he'd received word that William had died. He'd broken his neck in a riding accident.

It was at that point that Matt had been summoned by his grandparents. William's death had made him "the heir." They demanded his company. They had expectations for him.

He'd not obeyed instantly. He'd had mixed feelings about his grandparents and his role in the succession of the title. His loyalty was to his sisters and his parents' memories. Again, it had been

Alice who had prodded him forward. Mayfield was his birthright, she'd said.

Matt often wondered if his father would have agreed with her.

And yet, Matt had been curious about this mysterious world of the *haut ton*.

Now, he knew more than he wished.

Minerva frowned at the floor before muttering, "I thought you were here at Mayfield nursing your wounds and pining over Letty Bainhurst." There were actually tears in her voice as if he had betrayed her in some way. "You'd made quite a cake of yourself over her."

"I did." He could admit that much. Matt and Letty Bainhurst, wife to one of the most powerful men in England, had been lovers. In fact, he'd even thought of asking her to leave her husband and run away with him. He would have given up the title for her.

Or had he just wanted a love like the one his parents had enjoyed? A love that defied all conventions?

In the end, Letty cut him off. She'd suddenly refused to speak to him. She'd ignored his calls, his letters, his entreaties . . .

And that was the true reason he'd agreed to marry the Reverly Heiress. If the woman who owned his soul would not have him, well, then what did it matter whom he married? Of course, the decision hadn't set well with him. The day after his betrothal party to Willa, he had slunk away to Mayfield because in London he *was* a fool.

It had helped to leave. Once he'd stopped pitying himself, he'd started to perceive that what his grandmother had told him about the state of Mayfield's financial affairs did not equate to what his own reasoned intelligence noticed. He'd started asking questions. It had taken time to receive answers.

"What happened to the money?" he repeated to his grandmother. "What is the story? Was my uncle William involved?"

The mention of William stirred her. "He knew nothing about it." She straightened her shoulders. "And I shall not say another word."

"Then I won't marry the Reverly Heiress."

That robbed her of her starch. "You must. You can't abandon her at the altar."

Matt shrugged.

"There will be nothing if you don't marry her. You'll be ruined."

"*We'll* be ruined," he countered.

She pressed her lips together tightly.

"Don't make this so difficult," he said.

From somewhere in the house, he could hear the chime of a clock. It was not yet noon . . . and then his grandmother's face crumpled as if she could no longer hold in the truth.

"A man named Hardesty was blackmailing us."

Out of all the possible scenarios, that was one Matt had not anticipated. "*What?*"

"Blackmail," she repeated impatiently. "You know what that is."

"How could anyone blackmail my grandfather?" The old duke had been a stickler. He'd lived the upright, moral life. Matt had been trying to shock Minerva when he mentioned his grandfather and whores in the same sentence.

She removed her gloves with a distracted air, as if suddenly unnerved. "This man, Hardesty, he learned a secret. We paid him to be quiet. We had to. We had no choice."

Matt knelt by her chair and took her hand. Her fingers were cold. She started to shake. "Grandmother, it will be all right."

"It hasn't been 'all right' since that terrible man started sending letters. He always wanted more."

"Who is this Hardesty?"

"We never knew. He'd demand money and tell Henry where to leave it. We could never catch him even when Henry hired men to go after him."

"But why would you pay Hardesty?" That was the true mystery.

"For silence." Her fingers squeezed his tightly. She looked away.

"Grandmother, tell me."

"I wish you'd let this go—"

"But I won't. Tell me."

Her pale blue eyes met his. "Hardesty knew some uncomfortable things about William that he threatened to expose." William, the favored son. The heir.

A little over sixteen months ago, he'd died in a riding accident. He'd been out in the early morning and had been thrown. His neck had been broken.

Both of Matt's grandparents had taken his death badly. His grandfather's health had started failing immediately. In their last interview together, Henry had let Matt know that he considered his grandson barely a shadow of the man William had been.

"What uncomfortable things did he know about my uncle?" Matt had not known his uncle well, but by any account, William, Marquis of Tilbury, had been widely respected and admired. A true Corinthian.

Minerva drew another long breath. Her whole manner stressed how difficult the subject was for her. "William was a *complete* gentleman."

"Aye, he was."

"Except he had *unusual* tastes." Minerva looked at Matt as if gauging whether he understood what she was saying. "He would never marry. He was not of that persuasion to take a wife even though he was the most *masculine* of men."

Matt understood *exactly* what she meant.

The *ton* were a licentious lot. Depending on the tolerance of one's spouse, adultery was given a passing wink. There were great ladies who didn't know the true father of all their children. As long as they delivered a decent heir, their husbands were usually too busy with their own adulterous pursuits to care. Gambling wasn't considered a sin, even when a fortune was lost and children went hungry. Excessive drinking to the point of being incapacitated was more the rule than the exception.

But there was one vice for which a man could be successfully blackmailed—the "unnatural" crime. Any man could be imprisoned for it. Certainly, he would have been ruined whether he was a yeoman or a duke.

"Did my uncle tell you this himself?"

"No, but a mother knows. For a long time, I didn't believe Henry knew or suspected about William. However, after Hardesty started his terrible threats, and once Henry confided in me . . . then we understood that we both had known. I loved my son. I admired him. He was a worthy man in *every* aspect," she added, as if insisting on the fact.

Matt could have pointed out that she'd had *two* sons. William was the golden child while Matt's father, Stephen, had committed an unpardonable sin in the family—he'd married beneath himself. Or was it that he had ignored his father's dictates?

"How did the blackmail start?" he asked his grandmother.

With her secret out, Minerva had regained some of her composure. "Henry received a letter with reports of William's activities and a threat to go to the authorities. You know that if they received a complaint, they would have had to act. The scandal—well, it quite boggled the mind. We wished to protect William. Mayfield actually was beginning to have financial difficulties. The fields weren't producing. Money had been spent unwisely. Your grandfather had a desire to breed a great racehorse and had spent a fortune over the years in pursuit of that dream. Of course, it never happened. Breeding is tricky. It was all such a challenge, and then the horrid letters started coming. Henry paid to shut the man up. In the beginning, the amounts Hardesty wanted were small. Eventually, he always wanted more. And he kept sending his terrible reports."

"Did William know about the blackmail?"

She looked stricken. "He found out."

"How?"

Minerva bowed her head. She'd started pulling on one of the gloves she held. She stopped before confessing, "I told him." She lifted her gaze. Remorse filled her eyes. "I began to believe that Hardesty *controlled* Henry. Your grandfather was obsessed with preventing anyone from hearing the truth. It wasn't right. I lost my temper. I decided William should know. He would put an end to it. I *knew* he would."

"What did my uncle do when he learned of all this?"

"He was furious. He considered it an affront to his honor."

"Did he deny what Hardesty had accused him of doing?"

"No." She closed her eyes. "How I wish I had never said anything. Hardesty could have had all of Mayfield, but at the time—" Her voice broke off. Tears began to roll down over her cheeks. "I unleashed a horror upon us."

"Finish it, Grandmother. What happened?"

"I believe Hardesty murdered William."

Shocked, Matt stood. He took a step away and then came back. "Murdered? He broke his neck in a riding accident."

"There wasn't a horse in the world William couldn't ride. He'd never come off. However, shortly before he died, he told us he believed he'd discovered who Hardesty truly was and he was going to confront him. William's body was found close to one of the places Henry had left money for Hardesty."

"Did William go after the blackmailer alone?" That seemed particularly foolhardy.

"Apparently. He was alone when he was found."

"Was the magistrate notified of your suspicions?"

"It appeared an *accident*," she stressed. "We would have looked silly lodging a complaint of murder. And we wouldn't have told him anything about William's . . . life. And we *won't*." A touch of the autocratic dowager colored her last words. "I'll not let anyone sully my son's reputation."

Matt raked a hand through his hair, trying to make sense of something that seemed almost fantastical. "The blackmail stopped?"

"Yes, after William died. We wouldn't have paid another shilling . . . if we'd had it."

Matt paced the length of the room, trying to process all that he'd heard.

"Henry blamed himself for what happened to William and he was furious with me," Minerva admitted. "His heart couldn't stand the betrayal and I lost him." She appeared every year of her age and more.

Matt had nothing to say.

She looked to him. "But what's done is done. It is over. Honor was everything to Henry. As it was to William. And now, it is up to you to save Mayfield."

"By marrying the Reverly Heiress." He curled his hands into fists at his sides. The world would judge Matt by his ability to rebuild Mayfield. The responsibility of such an overwhelming challenge weighed heavy on him.

"It is your role," she replied simply. "You are Camberly."

Yes, he was. A role his father had shunned. An unreasonable anger toward his sire rose in him as well. He was in this position because his father had fallen in love with Rose Billroy. He'd made the decision to free himself of the responsibilities of the Addison name and any claim to the title.

But Matt couldn't do that. He was Camberly. As Alice had claimed, the title was his birthright.

A new purpose formed in his mind, one he had a feeling his grandfather and uncle would approve. "I want to know who this Hardesty is."

Minerva jumped to her feet. "*No*, Matthew, please. We have not heard from the odious man since William's death. Let it be."

But he couldn't. "I would be interested in what George has to say about this."

"George—? Matthew, *it is done. It is over.* I pray no one ever finds out about any of this. The shame would kill me."

"I'm not of a like mind. This Hardesty is nothing more than a common thief and, according to you, a murderer. If there is a way to track him down and bring him to justice while also wringing the money out of his worthless hide, I plan to pursue it—"

A knock sounded on the door. "What is it?" Matt asked, annoyed.

"A letter just arrived by messenger for you, Your Grace," the maid said through the door. "I was told to tell you it is from Miss Reverly."

He walked over to the door. Throwing it open, he took the

folded missive from the maid, who said, "The messenger said Miss Reverly does not need him to wait for an answer."

Frowning, Matt looked to his grandmother, who was very interested in the letter. "Thank you," he murmured, and shut the door. He cracked the seal, but his mind wasn't on missives from his "betrothed." No, he was thinking of how quickly he could hunt down this Hardesty.

And then his plans changed as he skimmed Miss Reverly's letter. She actually had a lovely hand. He had thought her writing would be awkward and full of the silly loops that women often favored to make their handwriting distinctive. Miss Reverly's penmanship was highly readable and her style direct.

"What does she have to say?" Minerva asked.

"She says she is releasing me from my promise—"

"She is jilting you?"

"Apparently." He found himself surprisingly displeased. Yes, he was angry about the marriage, but he did not like receiving the boot.

Especially in such an abrupt manner . . . and after *he'd* started to warm to the idea of marrying her for her much needed money.

Minerva stamped around in a worried little circle. *"She must not do that.* You have to stop her. You must go to her at once and tell her that she can't cry off. If you let her jilt you, you'll be tainted. Heiresses of her wealth are not common. Everyone will wonder what is wrong with you. They will ask questions. There are already whispers, what with you and Letty."

She'd said the magic words. Matt had no desire for Letty to know that another woman had found him lacking.

"I will ride to London immediately," he said, already moving toward the door. It was half past eleven. He could be knocking on Miss Reverly's door before four.

"I'll be right behind you," Minerva promised. "We must have a wedding, Matthew. Everyone in London is expecting one."

Chapter 2

Willa Reverly was blessedly thankful for the knock on her bedroom door.

"Miss Willa, the Countess of Dewsberry is here to see you," Annie, her Irish maid, said through the door.

"Bring her up immediately," Willa said, rising from her desk and the stack of papers she'd been staring at for hours in a vain attempt to make sense of her life now that she'd ruined it. For all her intentions, she'd written two things. The first had been the early morning message to Camberly ending her betrothal. The second was her desperate plea thirty minutes ago to her dear friend Cassandra, begging her to come *at once or I shall go quite mad.*

"And have the tray of sweets I ordered brought up," Willa informed the door. "Be certain there is cake."

Because cake always made things better. Or, at least, cake made *her* feel better.

Willa crossed over to the looking glass. She wasn't at her best. She pinched her cheeks, trying to put color in them, and pushed in the pins that had come loose from her heavy hair that had been twisted into a coil at the base of her neck. That was when she noticed she had ink stains on her fingers from her two letters and hours of toying with her pen trying to decide what to write.

She hurried to the washstand to scrub them off.

Her bedroom was as opulent as any room in a palace. Thick carpets covered the floor. The drapes were made of the finest stuff in blues and greens. It was a restful room and one that Willa, Cassandra, and their other friend, Leonie, had enjoyed over the years when they'd gathered to hash out the ball the night before or to complain when parents were being unrealistic in their expectations.

One of their chief frustrations had been being dubbed the Spinster Heiresses by the gossips. Was it their fault their fathers had enough power and wealth to demand only the best, *titled* husbands for their daughters? Husbands meeting their demanding standards weren't just ripe for the plucking. It took time and effort to attract such attention. Consequently, the friends had lingered on the Marriage Market for three long, interminable Seasons. Hence, the nickname Spinster Heiresses.

In truth, each father had turned down numerous offers for his daughter's hand because they could afford to do so. Leonie's father had been a rich nabob. Cassandra had been the heir to the Bingham fortune. Willa, whose father was the financier Leland Reverly, was the richest of them all and her parents' only child.

Now Leonie and Cassandra were both married and, surprisingly—and of interest to Willa—happily so. They loved and respected the men who were their husbands. That had given her hope for her own happiness—until the Duke of Camberly had destroyed all her romantic notions.

The irony was he had been considered the prize of the Season. Every marriageable young woman had wanted him. They had stalked him. Laid traps for him. Flirted and engaged him in every way possible.

And Willa had caught him.

Except, this morning, she had thrown Camberly back—

There was another knock. Willa flew to the door and threw it open. Cassandra was there, looking golden and radiant.

The two friends were a study in contrasts. Most men had to look up to Cassandra to meet her eye, and she was as fair as a field of grain.

Willa, who was dressed in a gown of the palest rose edged in finely fashioned lace, and shoes with the slightest hint of a heel, feared there were hitching posts taller than she. She could claim to be five feet if she held her head up really high, and wore small heels.

Her hair was a rich, dark brown, and so heavy and weighty, it was the bane of her existence. She spent hours brushing and braiding and it took as many as fifty pins to style. She dearly wanted to crop it short in the latest fashion, but her father refused to let her cut so much as an inch off.

And what her father wanted, the household, including Willa, was expected to obey.

"I'm thankful you've come," she told Cassandra as she pulled her into the room. Annie and a footman followed with a tray of cakes and strongly brewed tea and milk.

"Willa, what is it? Your letter—" Cassandra started before Willa warned her to silence with a finger up to her lips. Cassandra immediately stopped speaking, her blue eyes a bit surprised and confused that this would be one of *those* conversations.

In the past, Willa had been the one her friends confided in. She rarely had secrets . . . but she had one now. Except her secret would not be kept quiet for long. Too soon the world would know what she'd done.

The two friends awkwardly waited for the servants to finish their duties and leave.

The moment the door shut, Cassandra demanded, "What has happened? Your letter said you needed me for the 'direst' of reasons."

"Sit here," Willa said, directing her to the pair of chairs before the cold hearth. The refreshments were on a table between them. "Are you feeling well?"

Cassandra had shared only yesterday that she believed she was with child. The only other person she'd told besides Willa was her husband, Soren, because that was how close the two friends were.

"I'm fine. I barely show at all, and thankfully so. I would not wish to miss celebrating your marriage with you." Unlike Leonie, who was advanced enough in her pregnancy that she'd been advised not to travel.

"I would not have noticed if you hadn't told me." Willa picked up a small footstool and started to place it under Cassandra's feet, until she realized her friend had no trouble reaching the floor, unlike her.

Nor was Cassandra to be put off. She caught Willa's arm and gently tugged it for her attention. "What is it? Why did you summon me so urgently?"

Willa slowly stood, the footstool and cake tray forgotten.

"I have *broken* my betrothal to the Duke of Camberly."

Cassandra stared as if Willa had spoken gibberish. And then she sat back in the chair, her head tilting. "Beg pardon? Did you say you *ended* the betrothal? The one where you are having the wedding *tomorrow*?"

Willa nodded.

"The *betrothal*," Cassandra pressed as if still uncertain she understood, "that has your servants rushing around preparing for a wedding breakfast? An event that will be *the* talk of London? The whole reason Soren and I ventured from Cornwall?"

Biting her bottom lip, Willa nodded again before whispering, "Yes, that one." She admitted, "I've broken it. I'm done." And with those last words came a heady rush of both amazement at her audacity and pride in herself.

"Lord, that feels so *good* to say," Willa declared. "I've sent him packing. I'm *finished* with him. I'm *free*." She spread her arms wide to declare to the room as a whole, "*I will not* be marrying Camberly, who is too full of his own consequence to give *me* any of his important time. I've shown him what's what."

However, her friend's response was not as Willa had hoped. Cassandra's mouth opened, but she appeared too stunned to speak.

Willa filled the void, albeit with less exuberance than her previous declaration. "I know giving the duke the boot is completely out of character for me. I almost can't believe I've been so daring. I've surprised myself. Why, I'm almost as strong-willed and unpredictable as you or Leonie."

And then, Cassandra found her voice. She sat forward in the chair. "You are not serious? Please tell me you are *not* serious?"

"But I am. I had a messenger deliver the letter this very morning. There will be no wedding."

"No wedding? On the morrow? Oh, Willa. Willa, Willa, *Willa* . . ." Cassandra stood, her movement so abrupt, she almost knocked over the table with its cake and teapot. She caught the table before it could fall, steadied it, and then sat back down. "You *jilted* a duke? A *day* before you are to marry him?"

Annoyed by Cassandra's reaction, Willa said primly, "That is one way of seeing it."

"I believe that is the *only* way of seeing it. And your father approved of this?"

Willa took the chair opposite Cassandra's. She folded her hands in her lap, squared her shoulders, and admitted, "I haven't told Father yet. I will," she hurried to add. "But, frankly, I'm a bit surprised by *your* reaction."

"I'm definitely *stunned* by your actions."

"*You* make it sound terrible. I'm not 'jilting' him. I just *released* him."

"Released, jilted. They are both not good words. At least, that is the way the world will see it. Camberly asked you to marry him and you said—"

Willa cut her off with an impatient noise. "Camberly *never* actually asked me for my hand. He talked to Father, and Father accepted for me. I wasn't even consulted."

Cassandra leaned forward. "Did you not attend your betrothal party? The one with two hundred in attendance? Soren and I heard about it even in the wilds of Cornwall."

"I was there."

"Willa, why did you not speak up then if you didn't wish to marry him?"

There was the crux of the matter.

"You know how it is, Cassandra. It was flattering to receive an offer from the man all the other debutantes wanted. And the marriage pleased Father. I was hoping for the best."

"He will not be pleased when he hears this news."

Cassandra was right.

"I know it is hard to speak up, but, Willa, by agreeing to the betrothal, you gave your word, your family's solemn promise."

"Except Camberly is nothing like the man I believed him to be."

"What do you mean?"

Willa stood. She crossed over to the chest of drawers and opened the top one. From beneath some folded clothes, she took out a slender book and walked back to her friend.

"A book, Willa?" Cassandra half laughed her surprise. "You were not much of a reader."

"I'm not illiterate. I just don't carry on about them the way you do. However, this one touched me. It captured my imagination."

Cassandra reached to take the book. "I know you are not illiterate," she said as if in apology and opened to the title page, but then words failed her. Her expression turned incredulous. She looked up. "This is Camberly's book of poems. You found it."

When the new Duke of Camberly had first been introduced to London, everyone had scrambled to find a copy of *Love Fulfilled* written by Matthew Addison. He'd penned the poems when he was in university and a nobody. Consequently, very few volumes had been published.

However, once he'd been named duke, there hadn't been a woman in London who hadn't wanted to read it. The city had been full of rumors of how the poems had laid bare the young and handsome Camberly's heart.

Cassandra reverently turned the pages. "I tried everything to find it. How did you manage?"

"Father's money." Willa took her seat, crossing her arms tightly against her waist. She sat on the edge so her feet touched the floor. "That book is why I agreed to marry Camberly. I mean, he called upon me perhaps twice before he and Father agreed to a marriage. It was all very quick. However, I had read those poems, and for the first time, someone's words spoke to me. There is kindness and compassion in them. He talks about how true, everlasting love is a haven in life. And a man in love owes his beloved his honesty, loyalty, *fidelity*. I believed Camberly the man was the same as Camberly the poet."

"He must be," Cassandra answered soberly. "He wrote them."

"He couldn't have," Willa responded. "I'll never believe it. The duke is *nothing* like the poet. And I expected you to be more understanding."

Cassandra closed the book. "I wouldn't be your friend if I didn't give you my honest advice. Willa, what you have done will more than make your father angry—"

"Oh, he will be furious." Willa was not looking forward to that conversation. She tapped her toe impatiently.

"As he should be. This path you are taking will ruin you. It won't be terribly kind to Camberly, either. And it doesn't make sense because, let us be fair, you, Leonie, and I would have done anything to land such a catch only months ago. You won him. You will be his *duchess*."

Willa untightened her arms and aimed a punctuating finger at the book. "I don't want to be a duchess. What I wanted was the man who wrote that poetry. That man is attentive and kind. He respects women. He values the people in his life. Camberly himself has proven he is not *that* good of a catch."

Cassandra began ticking off the reasons she was wrong. "He has an enviable title—"

"There are better titles," Willa muttered. She reached for an iced cake off the tray. Eating cake always calmed her nerves.

"He is handsome—"

"I can't quibble over his looks. He turns female heads wherever he goes. I haven't met one yet who didn't *ogle* him."

"You are jealous," Cassandra noted, as if it was a mark in his favor.

"I am not," Willa insisted. "Women can stare at him all they wish."

"Some have done more than stare."

"You are speaking of Lady Bainhurst." Willa's appetite left her. She set the cake back on the tray. "I'm not pleased about that."

"I don't blame you. He was besotted with her. But I was under the impression she gave him his marching orders weeks before your betrothal. Is he still trailing after her?"

"I don't know. Her name was linked with someone else's, but they say her husband is watching her closely. Father insisted on inviting them to the wedding breakfast. He adores currying favor wherever he can."

"Lord Bainhurst is quite powerful, but still, to have *her* here on your wedding day?"

"I know." Willa shrugged her opinion. "Thankfully, they are out of town and not scheduled to return."

"Then that means Camberly *hasn't* been around Letty."

"I don't know if he has or not." The subject made her physically ill. Cassandra had set the book on the table by the tray. Willa had a strong desire to knock it to the floor. She stared at the cover as she said, "Letty is married. An honorable man respects those boundaries. I find it disgraceful. Disgusting, actually. If I hadn't read those poems, I would have seen Camberly sooner for the man he is."

Cassandra sat quiet.

Willa met her eye. "I don't want to marry someone like my father. He disrespects my mother with the women he keeps. Please tell me Soren does not do this. Would you tolerate it if he did?"

"I would skewer him on a spit and roast him alive if I caught him behaving like your father."

Willa nodded. "I fear I'd do the same thing. You worry that I'm ruining my reputation with this decision. I believe I'm rescuing myself from being charged with husband skewering."

"The law does frown on it," Cassandra had to agree with a smile.

"Pity," Willa answered. "I think my mother would have enjoyed skewering my father years ago. Now she just ignores him. After all, it is what is expected, but her life seems so empty."

"Many women take on their own lovers."

"You and I have always agreed that it seems a shabby way to live."

Cassandra nodded and returned to her list. "Finally, I must remind you that the duke is *young*. Young, titled, and very, very handsome."

"And broke. You forgot he barely has a shilling to spare."

"Yes, but you have plenty, and your father is determined to use his money and his power to marry you to a title." Almost gently, she pointed out, "He *will* marry you off, you know, one way or the other. With or without your permission. You could find yourself with worse than Camberly. You could be married to the Marquis of Ellmore who is in his dotage and impossibly crotchety. I can't imagine seeing him naked."

Willa's mind revolted at the image as well.

"Or to the Viscount Longford, who I hear is looking for a mother for his twelve children. They also say he is anxious to breed an even twenty." Her voice dropped to a whisper to add, "His first and second wives died in childbirth, poor women."

Children were an uncomfortable topic for Willa. Last week, she'd overheard her mother's friends speculating about whether a woman as petite as Willa could successfully bear the child of a man as big as Camberly. Their prognosis, and the stories they had shared with one another, had been alarming.

And it was a cruel way to die.

However, Cassandra's reminder that her father *would* marry her off was sobering.

Leland Reverly never left an asset untapped. A daughter was definitely to be used for his advantage.

Willa shifted in her chair. "Do you know what I've been doing since I sent that message to Camberly this morning? I've been trying to consider what I wish to do with my life. I mean, ever since I can remember, my sole purpose has been, as you point out, to marry well. But shouldn't there be something more in life?"

"What do you mean?"

"You are starting a school. You've always had a dream to create new ideas and now you are doing it."

"But that is just the person I am."

"Did you know Leonie is becoming an authority on roses? Lady Vickery was telling me she'd sent a cutting of one of her prized bushes to Leonie."

"She's written about her interests in her letters to me," Cassandra answered.

"You both have purpose. You are clever and you do meaningful things. What can I do?"

"You are very good at needlework. Far better than I am."

"Ah, I can darn socks."

"Don't mock it. Sock darning is an important skill for most of us."

"But not a rich man's daughter." Willa shrugged. "Servants have always taken care of matters for me."

"Interests will come to you," Cassandra said soothingly, "once you start living your life."

"I don't know if that is true. I have a deep fear that there is nothing of substance about me. I spent most of this day trying to imagine what I could devote myself to."

"And what did you decide?"

"Nothing," Willa answered. "The paper on my desk is blank. It is as if I can define myself only in terms of attracting a husband. It is all that has ever been asked of me. I offer nothing else to the world."

"You are being too hard on yourself."

"Perhaps I haven't been hard enough."

Cassandra leaned forward, reaching a hand out to her. "Willa, you are a strong, vibrant woman. You will find your meaning in time."

Willa wasn't certain. "If I don't I shall be like Kitty Pakenham."

Cassandra wrinkled her forehead. "Kitty Pakenham? Isn't she the General Lord Wellington's wife?"

"Finally! He'd promised himself to her ten years before he actually showed up to marry her. She said he asked and then he disappeared and left her alone. For *ten* years," Willa had to repeat.

"Wellington didn't really disappear," Cassandra said reasonably. "Wasn't he in the military all that time? He was quite busy fighting for our king. She knew where he was."

"If he was going to go dashing off, he shouldn't have extracted a promise of marriage from Kitty, leaving her to *wait*. I swear, men have all the fun."

"He was shot at, and war is ghastly."

Willa shook her head. "So is standing around ballrooms *waiting* for someone who you want to believe cares about you to put in an appearance. And Wellington hasn't been completely alone while he's been shot at. You know his reputation—even married."

"He is not the most attentive of husbands."

"Exactly. Just like my father and so many others. The men go off into life while the women . . . wait. And for what? Death?"

"You are being a bit dramatic," Cassandra warned.

Willa came to her feet. Pent-up frustration moved her to pace the room. It was also a blessing to finally be able to speak her mind to someone she trusted. She had her own list to tick off. "Camberly left right after our betrothal ball. It was as if the clock chimed midnight and he vanished. That was months ago, and it was the last time I saw him. We danced three times, he walked me around the garden, and then he was gone. He didn't even say good-bye. He just disappeared and then word comes to me that he is at Mayfield."

"Has he at least written?"

"No, not even to tell me he is alive. I feel like a dairy cow he has purchased. He has contracted a sale with my father and plans on showing up tomorrow to milk me. One doesn't write letters to dairy cows."

Cassandra choked back laughter. "That is a terrible image."

"A humbling one."

"It is, and surprising. Matthew Addison is one of my husband's friends. Soren speaks highly of him. I can't believe he'd be so . . ." She paused as if searching for a word.

Willa supplied one. "Thick?"

"I was going to say absent."

"Yes, he has definitely been that. Then my path crossed Lady Wellington's. Kitty saw me wandering around ballrooms alone and took pity on me. She said I reminded her so much of herself."

"Why were you wandering?"

"Because I don't fit in anywhere. Usually, once one is promised, you attend events with your intended. I was alone. *Obviously* alone. I am no longer one of the debutantes. I have my duke. If I was around them for the simplest of reasons, their mothers hissed at me like old geese, as if I will chase away prospects for their daughters. I can't join the matrons. All they do is gossip and discuss their children and their husbands. Oh, Lord, how they carry on."

"There are other women at these events than in those two groups."

"A single woman cannot roam around the card room."

"Isn't your mother usually there?"

"You know how she is with her friends. She has also made it clear that now is her time. She no longer needs to chaperone me the way she did before I was promised. According to her, she's done her part—I've landed a husband." Willa's mother was not the doting sort. "And you know Father. Always too busy and important for mere ballroom floors."

No, he saved the best of himself for his mistresses, something Willa had promised herself she would never tolerate. Especially after witnessing how happy Cassandra and Leonie were with men who valued them . . .

And yes, Camberly's infatuation with the adulterous Lady Bainhurst had been a strong mark against him.

It still was.

"But certainly, you have friends," Cassandra protested.

"I don't. You and Leonie were my friends. The others . . . ? Even Lady Bettina distances herself from me now that I am to be married to a man she has let everyone know she'd wanted. She has said some ugly things."

"I don't doubt it. She was always whispering about us."

"Until we brought her into the game," Willa reminded Cassandra. "The other evening, she informed me I shouldn't even be seen in Society without the duke since I had 'won' him."

The game had been a way for Willa and her friends to save themselves from boredom and to make light of the tedium of courting. Leonie had devised it. A suitable male of their choosing was singled out as the prize for the Season, and points could be earned for different actions of successful flirting. Being introduced to the gentleman was a point. Being asked to dance, three points.

Cassandra smiled ruefully at the memory. "You are right. She was eager to play, especially at flirting with Camberly. As I remember, you scored the highest points the year before with Lord Stokes. He was anxious to marry you."

"Until his mother caught wind of his plans. His family didn't approve of my family, no matter how much money Father has. However, Stokes was nice man."

"He was a bore, Willa."

"Very well, he was a nice bore. But he did pay attention to me."

"I remember you hiding from him once you realized how serious he was. Boring is boring," Cassandra assured her. "I'll also remind you that you won this Season's game, too. You do have Camberly—"

"*Did*," Willa emphasized, wanting there to be no doubt. "I have thrown him back, and I refuse to be sorry. It is the most liberating decision I've ever made in my life."

Or so she hoped. In truth, Cassandra's objections were giving her second thoughts.

"Society will not take kindly to your jilting Camberly, Willa,"

Cassandra warned, her voice commiserating. "You might be ostracized."

"Better to be ostracized than ignored."

"They are the same thing," her bookish friend pointed out.

"Oh, no, they are not. Being ignored is much worse. It means I don't matter. And I want to matter. I want to be important to someone, just as you are important to Soren."

"It might be hard to find a husband after basically leaving one at the altar."

"It might even be impossible. Father could even cut me off. Then I would have to darn my own socks. But I refuse to settle. I want what you and Leonie have found. I want a husband who doesn't mind my shortcomings." Something her father did not offer her mother. He was always picking at her perceived flaws. "I want a husband who will be my friend—"

"Yes, that is very important," Cassandra agreed.

"And I don't want to be lonely, not in my marriage. You know, Father treats me like a princess in that he is willing to buy anything I desire, and yet, since you and Leonie left London, most of my conversations are with the servants. This morning, I woke very early and realized I can't go through with this marriage. I don't wish to continue living this same life. I want to matter."

"Then you had best talk to your father and tell him what you've done."

Yes, there was that. "I will . . . when the moment is right."

"You exchange vows on the morrow," Cassandra said, as if prodding Willa's memory. "The house will be full of guests. The moment is now."

"We can still have the party . . ." Willa suggested meekly.

"Or Soren and I can have a coach waiting out front for when you tell your father and the roof explodes with his fury. We will whisk you away to Cornwall with us and you won't have to face the scandal."

The scandal. "Yes, there will be one."

"It is the price you will have to pay," Cassandra said.

"Mother will not be happy, either." Her parents would punish her for her defiance, and yet, Willa knew she would not back down. She couldn't—

A knock interrupted them. Annie's lilting accent said through the door, "Excuse me, Miss Willa, but you have a visitor. The Duke of Camberly requests a moment of your time."

The Duke of Camberly?

The title seemed to form in the air between Willa and the door. She rounded on Cassandra. *"He's here?"*

"Of course. After receiving your letter, I'm certain he will want answers. And, to be honest, you owe him an explanation. It is only right. Besides, you did wish his attention."

"I *wished* it two weeks ago."

"Willa?" Cassandra said patiently, her voice laced with the wisdom of experience. "Men rarely ever do what you wish, or expect."

Chapter 3

The trip to London had not been an easy one. The overcast day had given way to rain and mist, and the only horse available to Matt from Mayfield's stables had been a difficult mare with her own mind. Matt and the blasted animal had argued from the moment he'd left his stable door until the reins had been turned over to a street lad to keep the mare walking to cool her down.

So Matt was not in a conciliatory mood.

Especially toward females.

He had also not bothered to stop at his London home to change. He wasn't afraid to let Miss Reverly see him in his mud-splashed boots and breeches. Let her know that he had taken her letter seriously.

And he had.

Her terse wording was branded in his mind: *We are not suited. I am releasing you of any obligation to me. Sincerely, W. Reverly.*

What was she, a solicitor? She was releasing him with two sentences?

Miss Reverly's curtness was not how a woman should write to a man to whom she'd been promised. She hadn't minced words but had been clear she was willing to mince him.

The closer he'd come to London, the more he'd wanted to know *why*. What had *he* done to set her off? He hadn't even been in London since the evening of their betrothal party.

And now here he was cooling his heels in Reverly's palatial

London home that spoke of money and power. All the furniture was gilt-painted wood. There wasn't a worn carpet or threadbare pillow in sight. The air was scented with beeswax and the room showed the meticulous care of dozens of well-paid servants.

Gracing the walls were as many paintings as could be found in any stately house. A few were of landscapes or good horse-flesh. Most were portraits, although Matt doubted if any were of Reverly's ancestors. The man had supposedly come from humble roots, worked hard, and married well.

Matt suspected some of those paintings could have been those sold from Mayfield. Reverly was known to have a fondness for a bargain. He'd turn any agreement in his favor. "Greedy as a fox," one lord had warned Matt.

Well, God willing, the man would be his father-in-law.

Matt paced the length of the receiving room, struggling with his pride and temper and considering how best to approach the rebellious Miss Reverly.

Someplace in the house, footsteps could be heard. A clock chimed the hour. Late afternoon. He'd made good time from Mayfield.

A footman had taken his greatcoat and hat. However, his hair was damp. He combed it back from his face with his fingers just as he heard voices, feminine ones. He squared off with the closed double doors.

One half opened—and Miss Reverly seemed to float into the room.

For a moment, he was caught off guard. He'd forgotten how graceful she was. She reminded him of a petite opera dancer. Perfectly formed, no movement wasted, comfortable in her own skin.

And lovely. Far prettier than he remembered.

Four months ago, Matt had still been preoccupied with thoughts of Letty. Now, he was struck by what he hadn't noticed about his intended.

Yes, Willa Reverly was a mite of a thing . . . but there was something about her presence that made her seem taller and stronger than her size indicated. Dark, thick hair and clear skin made her conventionally pretty. What set her apart was the intelligence in her snapping blue eyes and the determination in her attitude.

For the first time, Matt realized perhaps one shouldn't underestimate an heiress.

She was not alone. To his surprise, Cassandra, Soren's wife, was with her. Any other time he'd be delighted to see her because this meant his good friend was in town.

However, now he struggled not to frown. He had no desire to have an audience for this interview. At least he liked Cassandra. Soren had chosen well. And yet, there was nothing he could do about the matter of her presence but play his part.

"Your Grace." Miss Reverly made the barest of curtseys.

He returned with the barest of ducal bows. They were as formal as strangers.

"Miss Reverly, you could put a garden full of flowers to shame." One thing Matt had learned about London ladies, they lapped up this nonsense. He truly believed it was impossible to overflatter one of them.

Willa Reverly disputed his theory. Annoyance and, yes, disappointment, crossed her face. "One should expect a better compliment from a poet."

So much for pleasantries . . . and his assumption that Willa was like all London ladies.

Riding had given Matt time to think and face some hard truths about himself. He had taken her sizable dowry for granted.

His sojourn in the country? Yes, it was true that Letty had broken his heart, except that, to be honest, he'd latched on to her because being named Camberly had been overwhelming. He'd never imagined he'd take on the title, even after his uncle had died. He'd naïvely assumed his grandfather would live forever. The old man must have thought the same or else he would have helped Matt become better prepared.

However, a blackmailer and a sharp-tongued heiress were waking Matt up.

Unfortunately, he was not liking Miss Reverly very much.

Perhaps because she was right? He *hadn't* given much thought to her. Guilty as charged?

He turned his attention to Cassandra. "How are you, Lady Dewsberry? Married life appears to suit you."

"It pleases me very well, Your Grace," she replied smoothly, with enough of a twinkle in her eye that he knew Willa had confided in her about the note.

Did that mean Willa had also spoken to her father? Perhaps Leland Reverly was even behind the message? If that was the case, there would be no dowry.

Keeping his smile determinedly fixed on his face, Matt said to Willa, "May we sit and talk?"

"I have said all I wish to say," was her rude reply.

"And yet, I apparently have much to explain." His voice sounded genial, but tight. It was the best he could manage.

"Why, Your Grace, I have no interest in hearing explanations."

She delivered her insults with a sweet, false smile, the sort of smile that meant she was furious with him—and that was good. Women never had strong emotions for things that didn't matter to them. His sisters had taught him that.

The time had come for him to take command.

To Cassandra, he said, "Would you excuse us, my lady? Miss Reverly and I require a private moment."

"Don't you leave this room, Cassandra," Miss Reverly countermanded. "*My* guests are not to be dismissed."

"Not even to discuss an issue of importance between *us*?" Matt asked. He attempted to sound polite. Instead, he came off testy.

"I've reached *my* decision. There is nothing to discuss."

My decision. Interesting, and hopeful. Her father might not be aware of what she'd done. "I ask that you hear me out."

"Your Grace, you may talk, but I will not listen."

"Then perhaps I should discuss this with your father?"

Her shoulders came back, her chin forward. "He has nothing to say to you."

"Then our conversation will be brief. I will have your butler ask him to join us." Matt took a step toward the door.

She stepped in his path. "He is not at home."

"He doesn't know about your letter, does he?"

Miss Reverly looked to Cassandra, who had an I-warned-you expression on her face. Matt decided the time was right to repeat his earlier request. "Lady Dewsberry, I wish a word with Miss Reverly."

"Yes, I believe that would be wise."

"Cassandra, *don't leave.*"

Her friend was already to the door. "I must, Willa. This is really between you and His Grace. My husband has taught me there are some conversations that should be private. But, please, give him a chance. Like women, men often do foolish things." She gave Matt a considering look and then shrugged her shoulders. "He might make a decent husband in the long run."

"Long run?" Miss Reverly echoed, her brows rising as if she couldn't imagine such a thing.

"It all depends on how quick he is to train. No husband is perfect," Cassandra allowed, and then added, conspiratorially, "If all else fails, the offer of our hospitality is still open. We will have the coach ready at midnight." With those words, she left the room, closing the door behind her.

"The coach ready at midnight?" Matt repeated, intrigued.

"You would not understand," Miss Reverly said dismissively. As if she was the queen of Sheba, she moved to the middle of the room and sat on one of the many brocade upholstered settees. "Speak your piece, Your Grace. Let us hurry through this. I have plans for the evening."

WILLA HAD LEARNED long ago that when one was petite and female, she'd best be willing to know her own mind. Especially since Society believed a woman shouldn't expect very much from life. That she was really little better than a bauble, a pretty ornament.

Well, Willa had learned from her struggle with blank pieces of paper that she had no desire to be the wife of a man who behaved as if she was merely a task on his tally list.

She had been honest with Cassandra—she yearned for what her friends had discovered, even though she wasn't quite certain what exactly that was. Or if she was even worthy of it. She felt pale and insipid when compared to the way her lovely friends took hold of life and found purpose in it.

Of course, after years of watching her mother, Willa knew she didn't want a man who doted on his mistresses more than his wife. That would not make her happy.

She was also discovering it had been easy to release Camberly from his promise when he wasn't standing in front of her. The duke was a good deal—no, a *great* deal—more handsome than she remembered.

In a capital filled with beautiful people, there wasn't a male in London who could be compared to him. Not in height or in dark, singular looks. Few had that square jaw that suggested character, or such a straight nose, or finely proportioned, even features. Even his ears were excellently formed, and Willa never admired ears . . . but she'd noticed, and approved of, his.

Camberly also did not need padding in his jacket. He had a horseman's build. His shoulders were broad and his muscles long. Her imagination did not rebel at the thought of seeing *him* naked.

She was also partial to deep blue eyes. Poet's eyes, Cassandra had once called them when she'd been half daffy in love with him herself. But then, Cassandra had always fancied poets.

Willa did not. Not any longer.

Or, at least, that is what she told herself, in spite of the strange fluttering in her belly at being in this room alone with Camberly.

His hair was damp. There was mud on his boots and breeches. He'd come for her, his costume said. He'd ridden *hard* to reach her.

Perhaps she was wrong about him—?

She quickly scrubbed the errant thought from her mind. One thing she'd learned from her father was that one must watch what men do, not what they say. The duke's absence had been too great an insult, and Willa did have her pride. She'd hear what he had to say, and then throw his words back in his face. She'd been quite successful so far in their interview. It was obvious Camberly didn't know what to do with her.

And then he surprised her. He left the room.

He shut the door behind him.

She found herself completely alone.

For the briefest moment, she debated going after him—

Oh, no, she would *not* follow after him. Even though she was brimming with curiosity—

There was a knock. Before she could decide to answer, the door opened. The Duke of Camberly swept inside, a pleasant smile on his oh-too-striking face.

"Miss Reverly, I'm honored you have a few moments for me." He sounded . . . sincere.

He shut the door and walked toward her. "Please, don't rise. Sit right there being your beautiful self." He bowed with a great deal more respect than he'd shown her earlier. "I have *pined* these last few months for the opportunity to see you again."

Ah, so this was his game: placating her.

Willa relished saying, "You have 'pined' for me? Pined? As if you were a tree?" She widened her eyes and batted her lashes, pretending to have bubbles for brains.

And he laughed.

The laughter caught her off guard. It was full-throated, strong, easy, and a far cry from the sound she imagined an arrogant duke would make.

He sat on the settee beside her and indicated the door with one hand. "Willa, I wanted to start again. I know I sounded silly, but sometimes being ridiculous is needed to break the tension."

Willa. He'd used her given name. It was the first time she'd heard it from his lips.

"I'm not tense—" she started to deny.

"Of course not. *I* am," he admitted freely, although that wasn't true. He seemed relaxed while . . . she *was* tense.

When she'd written her letter in the early hours of the morning, she had anticipated some sort of response. After all, he needed her dowry. Money was important. But she hadn't expected him to show up in person or so quickly.

If she'd thought about it, she would have anticipated manly bluster and stomping about. Or wheedling. Or he could have gone to her father to complain, but he hadn't.

He'd come to her first.

Was that enough?

She didn't know.

And she wasn't certain she'd wish to find out. She was not one to go back after she'd made her decision.

"Your Grace—" she started. However, he interrupted.

"I'm Matthew. Or Matt. I actually prefer the latter. It is how I think of myself and the name my family and friends use. My grandmother calls me Matthew. You can make your own choice." Without waiting for a response, he said, "I did not mean to ignore you after our betrothal—"

"You barely spoke two words to me before it," she had to interject.

He nodded slowly. "I believe matters transpired rather fast—"

"You actually asked my father for my hand. Not me. You didn't speak to *me*." She wanted to be certain he understood her full complaint.

There was a beat of silence. "I might have done that."

"*Might* have?" She faced him now, his offenses rising like bile inside her. "And everyone knew who you really wanted was Lady Bainhurst. That you were 'pining' for her. For all I know, the two of you have been carrying on scandalously over the past months while I have been left to wander around ballrooms like Kitty Pakenham."

"Kitty Pakenham?" he repeated in confusion.

"Never mind," she replied, not wishing to go into the details. "You won't understand. Men don't . . . because they can do whatever they wish. They can walk the earth as if they own it while expecting women to trail behind them, seeing to their needs and making their lives easier."

Oh, that felt good to say. Willa was almost in awe of herself.

And now she could barely breathe, waiting for him to deny and lie and chastise her. Because that was what men did. That was what her father did. They told women that what they could see with their own eyes was not true.

An indecipherable expression crossed his face. "I had hoped my friendship with Letty Bainhurst had been more of a secret."

"Everyone seems to know, except her husband."

"Probably because he has been with her for the past few months. I have not been with Letty. We did have a . . ." He paused as if not knowing how to characterize their liaison. "It was over before I offered for you."

So, rumors were wrong . . . ?

And then she heard herself ask a question she had promised herself she would never ask because she'd overheard her mother say it more than a time or two. "Do you love her?"

"I did."

Willa's stomach went hollow. She had not expected such frank honesty. Her father had always denied any emotions for any women in his life.

She made herself speak, "Well, then you should be happy that you are free to pursue her."

He reached for her hand. He was not wearing gloves. She wanted to refuse the contact but found she couldn't.

Other than the dance floor, the last time they had been hand-in-hand had been when they stood together in front of a crowded ballroom and announced their betrothal. They had both been wearing gloves then. Now, she was startled by how strong, firm, and warm his grip was.

"Letty claimed she was unhappy in the marriage. I was new to

London and the title, and obviously in over my head. I appreciated her attention. She offered me guidance . . . and I believed her when she said that I was her savior."

"She called you that?"

"Many times. Her husband didn't understand her. He didn't appreciate her. He ignored her."

"Then why didn't she live apart from him?" It was a question Willa had once asked her mother without receiving any meaningful response.

"Letty likes his money. And his power."

Of course. Her mother had once noted every woman could tolerate a great deal of unhappiness in exchange for a secure life.

Willa just didn't want to believe she was one of them.

She loved her father, but she clearly saw his shortcomings. She would not wish to be married to him.

"I was a bit of rebellion for Letty." There was bitterness in the duke's voice.

Willa tilted her head. Could a person be resentful over someone who no longer mattered? "They say Lady Bainhurst rebels quite often."

"I have heard." He straightened. "I wished to believe I was different. And isn't that what we all want?" he asked with a slight, deprecating smile. "To be uniquely valued?"

Yes, that *was* what she wanted.

"Listen," he said, claiming her attention and gently pulling her hand toward him, "I don't understand the reference to or even who Kitty Pakenham is, but I have sisters who would tell me that I have been an ass. I do owe you an apology. I lost my way. I became wrapped up in my own problems these last few months."

"You have sisters?"

"*Four* of them. And not one holds back on her opinion. They are brutally honest, much as I sense you are."

"I am not that direct, but I wish to be." That was true. His candor was a powerful lure for Willa. Her parents never conversed, not in the manner that she was talking to the duke—

Her mind stumbled over his title, and replaced it with *Matt. Matthew.*

Matt sounded right.

"I also believe," he said, "that we should revive that point game you and your friends played."

Her heart almost stopped in alarm. "The point game?" She attempted ignorance.

He straightened, even white teeth flashing in his smile. "Yes, the point game. Don't pretend you know nothing. You and your friends had a competition to gain my interest."

"You knew about it?"

"What was it, three points if I asked you to dance?" Matt said. "A point for an introduction? How many points did you receive when I invited you to a weekend party?"

"How did you find out about it?" Willa countered.

"Letty had heard—"

"Letty?"

He held up his hand as if to ward off whatever she was going to say. "I shouldn't have mentioned her. My apologies. However, the person-I-should-not-mention told me I had been singled out."

"*I* did not single you out. It was happenstance. You were the catch of the Season. The game always focused on one man."

"Why not all the others?"

"There is no sport in that," she replied.

"And you caught me." His voice took on a warmth. "Does that mean you 'won' the game?"

"I am not confessing to anything."

He gave her a wicked smile. "I wonder if *I* should play?"

Willa went on alert. "What do you mean?"

"To prove to you my attentiveness. How many points for a call?"

"Three."

"And for begging my intended for another chance?"

Their gazes locked.

"I don't know if we should give points for that," she answered, her throat suddenly tight. He sat closer than she had realized, and she did not mind.

"You are right," he agreed. "It shouldn't be a game." His gaze went to her lips, or was she staring at his? She couldn't take her eyes off them as he said, "However, will you let me try again? You have my complete attention now."

He certainly had hers.

There had been a time not so long ago when she'd dreamed about what it would be like for him to kiss her. There had been a line in one of his poems that had caught her attention . . . *My lover's kiss is like no other, an answer to my soul.*

Willa had never been kissed. Not once.

The night before their betrothal, she had anticipated he would kiss her. She'd practiced using the back of her hand. Her greatest disappointment had been leaving her own ball, still uninitiated in that practice that seemed the most common of all things between men and women.

But he could kiss her now.

Everything about him, from the laugh lines around his eyes, to the afternoon growth of his whiskers, to the scent of him, of horseflesh and rain and man, it all swirled around her, drawing her still nearer to him.

"Another chance?" his well-formed lips whispered. "Willa, will you marry me on the morrow—?"

The door opened.

Willa reacted by practically jumping to the other side of the settee and coming to her feet. Matt rose with more polish.

"Your Grace," her father said in his heartiest voice, and offered a bow. He was not a tall man. Both of Willa's parents were small in stature, but Leland Reverly could fill a room with the boom of his voice. "What a pleasure. No one told me you were here until just now." He looked between the duke and Willa and then grinned. "Having a moment, eh?"

There had been a time when Willa would not have been allowed to be alone with anyone. Her father sounded happy to throw her at the duke.

"We were just discussing the wedding, weren't we, Willa?"

She found herself nodding.

Yes. Yes, she would marry him . . . because she really hadn't known how to confront her father and risk his wrath . . . because maybe all she'd really wanted was a sign from Matt that he knew she was there . . . that she mattered.

And because she really wanted a kiss.

Was she being foolish?

She didn't know. But right now, it seemed like every muscle in her body, including deep-seated ones, hummed with awareness of him.

And it had happened so fast.

Desire surprised her with its intensity, with its willingness to trust.

"You know the invite to the wedding breakfast has been deemed *the* invitation of the year," her father said proudly.

"It will be a big day," Matt agreed. "Although for me, the prize will be Willa."

He spoke her name as if it was a caress. She remembered another piece of gossip she'd overheard—Letty Bainhurst claimed Camberly was a prodigious lover. None better, she said.

And Willa wondered exactly what Letty meant, even though her imagination sent heat to her cheeks and other regions of her body.

Matt took a step toward the door. "I should take my leave. I don't want to overstay my welcome." He looked to Willa on the last word, and she felt herself blush again.

He'd won her over. Effortlessly.

"Of course. Of course. You will see *plenty* of your bride after the morrow when you join the ranks of the rest of us poor husbands who find ourselves unable to escape the weight of the parson's knot." Her father laughed at his own jest and escorted Matt out into the hall, where a footman waited to help him with his oilskin coat, gloves, and hat.

Her father was beginning to say something else to Camberly when the corners of his mouth tightened. Willa moved forward so she could see what had displeased him. Her mother lingered in the hallway as if she had just come out of one of many rooms.

Joanne Reverly was a touch taller than Willa. She'd been a fiery redhead in her youth but now her hair had turned the color of a mouse pelt. She had a habit of staying in the shadows or tucked away in card rooms among her friends as if she didn't wish to draw attention to herself.

Her husband had always been the one to make the decisions. Her responsibility had been to carry out his wishes. Her acquiescence had never gained her his respect.

Willa walked down the hall and took her mother's arm. "Come, the duke has paid a call."

"That is nice," her mother answered, allowing herself to be directed to the gathering by the door. She gave a small curtsey to Camberly. "It is good to see you again, Your Grace."

"Especially under such happy circumstances, no?" he answered, pulling on his gloves.

"Ah, yes," her mother agreed. Her glance shifted to her husband. "All is good."

"It will be the affair of the decade," her father promised the duke. "It will be remembered throughout all of history."

The pleasant expression on Matt's face didn't waver, except Willa noted his gaze went from one parent to another with sharp scrutiny, and she wondered what he was thinking. Few people cared about the dynamic between Leland Reverly and his wife.

And Willa realized that if she had cried off, it was her mother who would have paid a price. Her father would have blamed her for Willa's rebellion. Willa was now thankful that Matt had eased her doubts.

Peters, the butler, held the front door open, but Matt eased closer to Willa. "I'm sorry we were interrupted." He spoke for her ears alone.

She was as well, but she didn't trust her voice to speak, not when her father was obviously straining to catch every word between them.

Matt took her hand. Lifting it to his lips, he surprised her by turning it over and kissing her wrist. His lips lingered there a moment, right upon her pulse, and she thought she might faint from the surge of heat that shot through her.

He met her eye and then smiled. "Six points," he whispered, reminding her of his intent to play the "game." His husky tone hummed through her body.

"Four points," she managed to croak out. "That wasn't worth six points."

His grin turned wolfish. "I shall take that as a challenge."

"I pray you do."

Where had that come from? She had started off so angry with him that she had been willing to risk scandal, to now counting the minutes until she would see him again.

He had convinced her to trust him. He'd slipped past her doubts and wariness. Although the impetus for their marriage was money, she was beginning to believe there *could* be something meaningful between them.

It had also not escaped her notice that when the servants had helped him with his coat, he'd murmured a thank-you. He was male, *and* he was appreciative?

Perhaps Camberly was different.

He released her hand. "Until the morrow, Willa. I shall be waiting for you at the church." With a cocky set of his hat, he was out the door.

She watched him toss the street lad a coin and gather the reins of his horse. The animal seemed hardly tamed, and yet, he was up in the saddle and on his way.

She placed her hand over her wrist where he had placed his kiss. She'd lied. It had definitely been worth six points.

My lover's kiss is like no other, an answer to my soul . . .

Chapter 4

*M*att had salvaged the marriage. Miss Reverly's much needed dowry would be his, and his grandmother could rest easy. He'd not be jilted on the morrow.

Then again, he'd not had a fear of that. Matt had known he could work his way around Willa. She'd had more to lose than he had. He could have found another heiress . . . but what sort of life would she have had if she had succeeded in rejecting him? He'd saved her from being branded an eccentric and toddled off to some nether place reserved for headstrong and foolish women.

Although his sisters would have applauded her on. There wasn't a one of them who would have approved of how Matt had treated Willa. And he did feel a bit ashamed.

As he rode through London's busy streets, Matt had to admit that Willa Reverly had caught him off guard.

In the past, when he'd called upon her, they'd not spoken on any topic with depth. It had not been necessary. She was a means to an end, a way to fill his empty coffers. She'd seemed poised enough to be a duchess, and that was all that one expected.

Besides, when compared to Letty, Willa had lacked fire. He'd convinced himself that would be fine. Preferable, even. Except he hadn't been excited or even truly interested in marrying her— until she'd threatened to jilt him that morning.

Now, it was as if he was noticing Willa for the first time. She was an attractive bit, and there obviously was a brain under all her hair. She had proven she had some spirit to her as well.

His mare kicked out as she passed an ostler leading two horses through the busy streets. "Sorry," Matt muttered in answer to the man's curses, and pushed the mare forward as his thoughts returned to his bride, and a decision.

Over his months at Mayfield, he'd vowed that he would never again let a woman make a fool of him the way Letty had. He would never again trust anyone so freely. He'd been too open with his heart, too caring, too bloody naïve.

No wonder he'd been such a terrible poet. And a foolish duke.

On the rare occasions when Matt had been with his grandfather, Henry had admonished him to not be "soft" like his father, Stephen. Both of his grandparents had believed that the actress Rose Billroy had bewitched Stephen into disappointing his family. Over the years, Matt had learned that they did not believe in the concept of "love."

"Hogwash and nonsense," Henry had declared when Matt had tried to defend his parents. "Love is lust in disguise. A forward-thinking man doesn't let himself be led around by his short staff."

Henry must have turned in his grave over the way Matt had tossed his heart at Letty.

However, Matt's marriage to Willa was one of convenience. For both of them. A simple business transaction that would have met with Henry's approval. Certainly, Minerva was pleased.

Matt would be a good husband to Willa. He would treat her fairly and with respect. In turn, she would have a position of authority in Society.

Nor was he going to mind bedding her. She was a tempting piece. Of the three Spinster Heiresses, Willa had been the one to catch his eye.

However, Matt was starting to think that, perhaps, his feelings for Letty had been nothing more than lust? Henry had once opined that if Stephen and Rose had lived longer, "They might have been as miserable as the rest of us. One can't sustain passion."

Certainly, Letty hadn't been able to sustain her feelings for Matt for more than sixty days.

And the truth was, Letty had broken him. Matt would never allow himself to feel for any woman what he had for Letty. He'd never give his heart again. Or his trust. That was where he'd gone wrong. He'd given too much.

He turned the mare onto High Holborn Street. The hour was half past four. Matt caught up with his cousin George just as he was leaving his chambers.

George Addison was at least twenty-five years older than Matt. They shared the Addison height, although Matt was inches taller. George's dark hair was now streaked with gray and his eyes were a trustworthy brown. In looks and manner, he reminded Matt of his own father, Stephen.

George's sire had been Matt's grandfather's twin, and the younger by a mere two minutes. Henry's favorite jest was that if George's father had been quicker, he'd have been the duke.

It was a poor joke. Then again, if George had any resentment, he never showed it. In fact, he'd always been kind to Matt. When Matt's father had died, George had been the only member of the Addison side to attend the small service. It was at the funeral that Alice had approached George about setting up a meeting between her and their grandparents. George could have refused, and then Alice, who had been newly married and starting a family of her own, would have found it difficult to gain an audience with Henry and Minerva.

Instead, according to Alice, George had championed her desire to see Matt properly educated. He'd helped sway Minerva and Henry's opinions. If his uncle William had a voice in the matter, Matt had never heard.

George had also taken Matt aside and urged him to study hard. "You never know which way life will go. Study a profession. Make yourself useful."

So Matt felt close to George. He valued his opinion. When Matt had inherited the title, George had supposedly shared everything he knew about the estate's affairs . . . everything except the blackmail. Matt was anxious to hear what he had to say.

George was surprised by Matt's appearance at his door but greeted him warmly. "Ah, so the prodigal duke has returned from the country. There *will* be a wedding."

" 'Prodigal' duke?" Matt winced. "Is that what they are saying?"

"What? Do you believe *I'd* coin such a phrase? But yes, it is whispered that you are licking lovesick wounds. There isn't a betting book in town that doesn't have a wager over whether you would show to wed the Reverly Heiress or not."

"Did you write down a wager?"

"A yellow George either way."

"Hedged your bet, eh?"

"Always. I'm a lawyer, Your Grace. It is how I make money." He then added slyly, "Have you heard the rumor that Letty Bainhurst asked one of her many male friends to place a wager on the matter?"

Matt grimaced. If he needed proof of what Letty truly thought of him, well, there was an answer. Doggedly, he focused his mind elsewhere. "How is Venetia?"

George was married to a woman who had been a renowned beauty in her time. However, Venetia had taken to her bed several years ago and rarely went out. George had once told him it was because of her melancholy nature. He and his children appeared devoted to her.

"Much the same," he answered. "I wanted her to attend Evanston's rout this Saturday with me. She might."

"You have always been good to her," Matt observed.

"That is marriage. You stand by your wife, your children, your family," he added with a nod to Matt. "You do what is right."

"Including paying off a blackmailer?" Matt asked.

George had been locking the door, but he now went rigid. His head turned to meet Matt's eye. "How did you learn of this?"

"I confronted Minerva."

"She wouldn't have told you on her own. She didn't want you to know."

"I found the money missing in the ledgers. It was actually quite obvious. Shall we discuss?"

George pulled the key from the door and pushed it open. "Come in." He followed Matt into the anteroom. It was filled with empty desks.

"Everyone has gone home early?" Matt observed. Usually the office was a hive of activity.

"My clerks? A few are on errands. Another I sent home. The lad appeared peaked and I don't want his sniffles around me."

George indicated that Matt should continue to his private chambers. Inside was a large desk covered with neat stacks of ledgers, much like the ones Matt had spent his time studying at Mayfield.

On the corner of the desk was George's wig and stand, a symbol of his profession. A large bookcase took up one wall, and the room smelled of paper, bindings, and ink. George waved Matt to a chair in front of his desk.

Matt took a seat and placed his hat on the desk next to the wig stand.

George removed his own hat and set it on the wig. He took his chair behind the desk. "Would you like a drink, Your Grace?"

Matt shook his head. "No, thank you." He needed his wits about him.

"You do not mind if I do?"

"Please, go ahead."

George took a glass out of his desk drawer. The building was quiet at this hour, just the way Matt would wish it. No prying eyes or unwanted ears. The day was ending. The street traffic outside spoke of people hurrying to their homes or rushing to other activities. The overcast skies had been clearing and a faded autumn light came in the window and highlighted George as he poured his drink. He placed the decanter to the side before saying, "What do you wish to know?"

Matt leaned forward in his chair. "Tell me what you know of Hardesty."

George looked away as if he would rather avoid the conversation, but then he said, "Hardesty is a criminal. My advice is that you steer clear of him. Or has he been in contact with you or the dowager?"

"No, we have not heard from him. Grandmother said that after William's death, they have had no further contact. Why did you not tell me about the blackmail?"

"Because it was the past. It was done."

"Except the man's demands bankrupted the estate."

"I told Henry to report Hardesty to the authorities when he first received the letters years ago. He wouldn't. Instead, he asked me to hire some men to hunt the bastard down and beat him senseless. Of course, no one could find him. The man is like a shadow. We found signs of him and heard whispers but could never catch him. Worse, anything we tried only made Hardesty demand more. Henry was afraid . . ." He paused and then carefully said, "You know about William?"

"I do. Did *you* know about Uncle William?"

George drained his glass and set it aside before admitting, "I had heard rumors, although most people didn't know, or so I believe. William was discreet. I will also say, he was a good, stalwart man. Ambitious, but honest. The last man one would believe of being—" His voice broke off. He looked to Matt. "I counted him a friend. He would have been a brilliant duke."

Much better than myself, Matt could have answered. After all, William had trained all his life for the role. He'd been the Marquis of Tilbury. He understood the expectations. He'd been discreet in his amorous pursuits.

Instead, Matt sat quiet.

Leaning his arms on his desk, George said, "I suggested, especially when I saw how determined this blackmailer was of draining the estate dry, that Henry tell Hardesty to have at it, let William's name be dragged through the muck. Your grandfather refused."

"He loved his son," Matt said. "Both of my grandparents did."

"More like he didn't want any scandal to taint the title and consequently himself. Henry was proud and vain. A stickler through and through. Look at what your grandparents did to your father. And to you before your sisters pushed you forward."

"Grandmother will still not recognize them."

"The duke and his duchess barely recognized you until William died."

That had been true. "They made me angry," Matt confessed. "They paid for my education but little else until I became the heir. I wasn't going to accept the title. I could have lived my life without it or them."

"What changed your mind?"

"My sister Alice. She's always the peacemaker. Of course, I thought once I became Camberly, then I could use the title's income to help their lives, educate their children. Thanks to Hardesty, there is nothing to share."

George poured another drink. "I didn't understand how Henry could be so cold, especially when your father died. He'd lost a son but he never spoke of it."

"Or attend the funeral."

George nodded. There was a beat of silence and then he said, "Venetia and I lost a baby. A girl. She was only five weeks old. I don't believe Venetia has ever recovered."

"I didn't know," Matt said. "I'm sorry to hear of the child's death."

"It was about the same time your father died. Hard for both of us," George answered, and took a healthy sip from his glass. He set it down, forced a smile. "But now things are better for you, no? You will marry the Reverly Heiress and set the estate to rights."

"That is my intention."

"Her dowry is so vast, you can even educate those nieces and nephews of yours. Of course, be ready, Minerva will not approve."

"My grandmother does not have a voice in the matter."

"And that is good. There is a fresh wind coming into the title. One that has a good head in these modern times."

Matt acknowledged the compliment but then said, "Grandmother believes this Hardesty was behind William's death."

George sat up in his chair with a start. "No . . . she's never said such to me."

"Was there anything suspicious about William's death that you knew?"

"Or that the magistrate noticed? I read the report, as did your grandparents. He broke his neck on one of his fool nags. He liked them spirited and silly."

"He was a known rider."

"Aye, he was a bruising one. I couldn't hunt with him. He'd jump anything when it would have been twice as easy to go around. He loved a risk, especially on a horse. But the fact is, sooner or later, you come up against something that has the better of you."

"So you don't believe he was murdered?"

"I believe that is the wish of a grieving mother. But it doesn't hold up. Why would Hardesty want to kill his pot of gold? Once William died, there were no blackmail demands."

"Which is a bit surprising."

"What do you mean?"

"My grandparents would have continued to pay to keep the story quiet. Their reputation, you know."

"Or they might not have. I would have advised them against it. There'd be gossip and a bit of scandal, but it wouldn't last more than a week." George finished his drink. "You know the whole story now. Fortunately, it is behind you. You are free to rebuild what was all but destroyed."

"At a great cost. And for that reason, I want justice," Matt said. "I need those men you once hired to search again for Hardesty. I want the estate's money returned."

George leaned both elbows on his desk. "That might not be possible."

"Then I'll wring the money out of Hardesty's hide."

"We don't know who he is. We could never find him."

"I want to try again."

George held his gaze a moment, and then shrugged. "You understand the sort of men I had to hire don't work without coin up front."

"I will pay."

"Thank God for heiresses, eh?" George leaned back in his chair, crossing his legs and half turning from Matt. "And there are no guarantees."

"Find me good men, true hunters. Set them loose."

George acted as if he thought better of the request, but then conceded, "It will take time, but I will do as you ask. I could weep over what has happened to Mayfield. I confess, I was worried when you took over. I knew what was going on and feared you would not have the stomach for it."

"I'm an Addison," Matt answered. "We do not let any slight go unanswered."

" 'Stand fast,' " George said, quoting the Addison family motto, the one created by the first Duke of Camberly.

Matt nodded his agreement and stood. "Thank you for your time, George."

His cousin jumped up from his chair and bowed. "It is my pleasure, Your Grace. I will see you on the morrow."

Matt offered his hand. The men shook on their agreement, and Matt left.

He was not surprised when he reached his home to find his coach at the front door. His grandmother had returned from Mayfield. Handing off the by now exhausted mare to a stable lad, Matt entered the house.

Minerva came into the hall from a side room. She held a brimming glass of sherry in her hands. "Well?"

"There will be a wedding on the morrow."

Her relief was obvious, and he understood.

Now that he'd stopped fighting the marriage, the weight of responsibility that had been his constant companion since he'd taken the title had fallen aside. His money worries would vanish. It was as if he could draw a full breath for the first time in what seemed ages.

That night, he enjoyed a rare beefsteak and a glass of whisky and embarked on a good night's sleep—until he woke in the middle of the night and realized he did not have a groomsman.

He had not performed this most basic of groom's duties, and it would be a telltale sign that he had not been interested in the marriage.

Matt jotted a quick note to his friend Soren, woke his butler, Marshall, to see that it was delivered, and then went back to sleep, convinced that he had saved himself from a major blunder.

WILLA HAD A terrible night's rest.

Part of the blame she placed on her hair. At night, she wore it in a long braid that was as thick as her wrist. When her body turned, the braid would sometimes be caught beneath her. She hated being woken that way.

Last night, it had happened several times, and whenever she woke, her mind would take over with a thousand thoughts.

Her life was about to change. For the past three and even more years, all anyone spoke of was the man she would marry.

And now the time was here. Her life was finally going to begin.

She was past ready. Staring at the medallions and scrollwork on her ceiling, she ruminated on how happy Cassandra had appeared. How content. Willa wanted to be that content.

Of course, she barely knew Matt. Her husband. His Grace. *Her* Grace. Her Grace. *His* Grace.

Her father was very pleased with her. Apparently, he, too, had been anxious about Matt's prolonged disappearance from London.

But now he was here, and in a matter of hours, Leland Reverly could proudly claim he had a duke for a son-in-law. Willa had no doubt that her father would even have calling cards made up that said, "Leland Reverly, father-in-marriage to the Duke of Camberly."

Furthermore, the whispers had not been true. Matt was not indifferent to her. He was going to marry her.

However, what the gossips thought was of no importance . . . because Matthew Addison, Duke of Camberly, *was* a prize in

Willa's mind. Points aside. He was tall and exceedingly handsome. Why, there wasn't a woman in London who didn't crave his attention. He moved with energy. He had all his teeth. He had all of his *everything*.

And he had come for her. He'd challenged her decision to release him from the betrothal. She wasn't naïve enough to believe that meant he cared, but at least he'd noticed her.

In the dark, she lightly rubbed the pad of her thumb over the place where Matt had kissed her wrist and added another characteristic of her own to Matt's tally of traits—he was kind. That was a sign of goodness.

He'd been angry when he'd first arrived. No, he'd been *irritated*. There was a difference. But he'd listened to her complaints, and she believed he'd genuinely heard her. After all, wasn't that what anyone wanted? To have someone who listened?

Last night, her father had stayed home. He'd joined her and her mother for a simple dinner. The kitchen had been too busy preparing the wedding breakfast that would be served shortly after noon on her wedding day. Kegs of ale and whisky had been laid in. Port, Madeira, sherry, and even French wines had been acquired. The actual ceremony at the church would be private and quiet, but, in her father's mind, the wedding breakfast was what mattered. It was his opportunity to display his power and wealth.

Therefore, for once he had not minded a boiled capon and buttered bread. Even her mother had acted pleased about the marriage.

Willa tossed her braid once more across the pillow and, curling up, tried to sleep again. Tomorrow, she would experience the marriage bed. Matt was rumored to be a powerful lover. A line from one his poems echoed in her mind: *Lost in her, deep within her, I find solace and grace.*

When she'd first read those words, she'd stared at them, trying to divine their meaning. They were both mysterious and earthy, as if the lover had special powers.

The man who wrote those words wasn't a man like her father, who flitted from woman to woman. No, Matt's poem told her that *his lover* mattered.

If that wasn't enough to keep a woman awake—?

Especially when she wasn't quite certain what all would happen.

She did fall asleep, because Annie woke her at half past seven with a breakfast tray. The house smelled of delicious food.

"You should see the rooms downstairs," Annie said, opening the drapes. "The footmen worked all night setting up tables. They came in by the cartloads. I helped with the coverings. Cream and gold. Mr. Reverly is sparing no expense. Not for his daughter."

Coming over to the bed, Annie gave her an indulgent smile. She had been one of the constants in Willa's life. She had joined the staff as a nursery attendant when Willa was five. At that time, it was said that Willa had been a terror. She hated for anyone to brush her hair, and few said no to her.

With patience and the practicality and good humor of the Irish, Annie had coaxed Willa into letting her tame her wild tangles. She'd done it by telling Willa stories of mice who enjoyed tea parties at night in little girls' hair. Willa still wished to believe any snarls and tangles were the result of too much treacle syrup.

Over the years, she and Annie had made a fast bond, although the maid knew her place. However, whenever Willa fell, Annie was there to pick her up. When the world was confusing, Annie helped her understand.

And when Willa needed to shine socially, Annie primped and ironed to be certain she did.

"Did you sleep all right?" Annie asked.

"Barely. My hair." Willa rubbed her eyes and yawned.

"It is more than just your hair that kept you up," Annie said with a twinkle. "You are about to become a duchess. Proud I am, Miss. Now, eat. A bath will arrive in a few minutes."

While Willa nibbled a hot bun and sipped chocolate, Annie

pulled from the wardrobe the wedding dress. It was of the whitest muslin, shot through with threads of silver and gold, and had capped sleeves. It was both innocent, and yet a touch enticing— which was the way Willa thought a bride should be.

The bath arrived with great ceremony. Even though the footmen had been up most of the night and would continue to be on hand this day, their spirits were high in her honor. They were going to be well rewarded for their hard work. There would be extra vails from not only her father but from the other guests.

Willa didn't dally with her bathing. Her stockings were of the palest silk and she wore white kid slippers. The shoes also had a small heel, so they added perhaps an inch to Willa's height.

Now that she was dressed, Annie sat her on a bench before the full-sized looking glass. "The pearls?" She referred to Willa's pearl-tipped hairpins.

"Yes, I believe so."

Annie fetched them and put them in Willa's hand so she could hold them while the maid went to work.

Thinking about how tall Matt was, Willa said, "I want my hair as high on my head as you can build it. Is there a comb or something we can use?"

"Let me try this." Annie wrapped a curl around her finger and pinned it into place with the plain pins from Willa's other hand. The maid took on the concentration of an artist sizing up her masterpiece. She built several curls on top of each other before adding the pearls. "I like this. You look like a goddess with your hair up. When the duke sees you, he will be smitten."

The last thing Annie added was a lace veil that trailed over Willa's shoulders and down her back.

When Annie was done, she motioned for Willa to rise. "You are the loveliest you have ever looked, miss." She reached down and pulled on the dress hem. "Everyone will be stunned to speechlessness when they see you. Especially the duke."

Willa couldn't imagine Matt speechless, but the idea pleased her.

Caught up in her own thoughts, Annie continued, "You and the duke will be very happy. I feel it in my bones. My nan was one who had the sight and I have a bit of her gift. Thinking of the two of you together, I receive the tingles."

"The tingles?"

"Yes, it is when there are little shoots of awareness all over me. I have the tingles when I think of the two of you together."

Willa laughed, enjoying the prediction.

A soft knock on the door interrupted them. Her mother entered without waiting for permission. She was dressed for the wedding in a deep purple gown. Her hair had been curled, and Willa thought she looked very handsome.

"Mother, what do you think?" Willa twirled.

"Very nice. Are you ready?"

"I have my gloves, and what is the weather? Can I wear a light shawl, or should I take something heavier?"

"It promises to be a perfect September day. The light shawl should suffice."

Annie went to the wardrobe and pulled out a cream paisley shawl and a yellow one made of lace. Willa chose the paisley. She did not like wearing lace on lace. She reached for the gloves Annie had laid out.

Her mother walked around the room as if nervous. She paused by the bed. "Annie, we wish a moment of privacy."

"Yes, ma'am." Annie ducked her head and left, closing the door behind her.

Sitting on the bed, her mother patted a space beside her. "Your father wondered if I'd had a conversation with you . . . about the marriage bed. He wants to be certain you know what to expect."

Finally. Heat rushed to Willa's cheeks, but she'd been waiting for this discussion. She and Cassandra had always speculated. Leonie had never wished to take part in such discussions. She had claimed to be too shy. But Willa was curious. Cassandra had promised her she would like it. Willa sat on the edge of the bed, ready to hear if her suspicions were correct.

Her mother drew a deep breath as if bracing herself. "Young women seem to know so much these days. I'm not certain what I need to tell you. What is it you know?"

"I know my husband expects me to share his bed."

"Yes, he will do that . . . for a while. Anything else?" Her tone was brusque. She didn't act as if she was particularly anxious for questions.

And yet, if Willa did not ask now, she might come off as silly or foolish to Matt. "I have a hazy idea. He'll want to *join* with me." The word had been another line from one of Matt's poems—*On a bed of roses, we joined, finding our peace in each other.*

"Do you know what that entails?"

"I've seen animals, Mother." She'd also caught an eyeful of behavior from time to time on the street that proper young women should not have noticed. "But is there something in particular of which I should be aware?"

Her mother's gaze drifted from Willa as if she wished she was somewhere else, and then her expression hardened. She faced her daughter. "It isn't complicated. Your husband will instruct you. It will hurt."

"Why will it hurt? I've never heard anyone complain of it."

"Because of what men do," her mother answered. "They stretch us. It's painful."

Stretch? Willa had also never heard talk of stretching.

"Your husband is a very big man. I fear you will experience great pain. You will bleed."

Now she had Willa worried. She knew about a virgin's blood, but "bleed" was more than a few drops.

"I *hate* it," her mother confessed, as if she could not prevent herself. "I've hated it from the very first. It is our curse to bear for being born female. I'm disgusted to think I even had to submit to it. It is vile and disgusting and *sticky.*"

Sticky? That seemed an odd, and unanticipated, description to Willa.

"No proper lady would enjoy it," her mother vowed. "But here is the secret, Willa—because men don't want their wives to complain or ask questions—I found that if I silently counted backward from one hundred, well, then it would soon be over and he would leave me alone."

"You just lie there?"

"Of course, there is nothing else you can do. Let the duke have his way with you, and no matter what, do not complain."

Willa swallowed. "Will I bleed every time?"

Her mother shook her head sadly. "It depends on how violent he is."

"*Violent?*"

"Men stir things up." She circled her hand over the region of her belly, an area far deeper into her body than Willa had imagined her husband would go. "It is not pleasant, Willa. No one has ever said it was. My friends and I are happy now that our husbands leave us alone."

Willa thought of the longing looks her mother often sent in her father's direction when he was going off for his own pursuits. Had she misread them? "Cassandra doesn't act as if she hates it." Then again, they had not discussed such intimate things since Cassandra married. Yesterday, they had been too busy talking about the letter Willa had sent.

"Perhaps she is with child? Men leave their wives alone once they are pregnant, for obvious reasons."

Those reasons weren't obvious to Willa. "The poets praise it," she offered.

"Poems are written by men. Of course they would praise it. They don't have to bring children into the world. They would change their tune if they did."

"But some women have more than one child. If it is so terrible, why?"

"Those poor women are not free to say no to the men they married. Or they can be the sort of coarse creatures *your father* prefers. Women who are not delicate and sensitive. I didn't raise you to be that sort." She reached out and touched Willa's hair. For a moment, she was the mother of Willa's childhood. "And I pray that birthing one of Camberly's babies doesn't cost you your life."

Willa almost fell off the bed at her mother's startling announcement. She leaned forward. "I overheard you talking to your friends about this. Why should this be a fear, Mother?"

"You are petite, Willa. It is a part of nature that a ram and his dam should be well proportioned to each other. Still, it is a worry for any of us. Mr. Jamerson at the lending library just lost his wife. The baby survived, but that poor woman did not."

"Poor Mr. Jamerson." Willa was fond of the young man who was always a help when she searched for a book. He found the duke's book for her.

"Yes, it is terrible. Childbirth is serious business."

"What of Cassandra? Or Leonie?"

"It can be a danger to them as well."

This was not news Willa wanted to hear on her wedding day.

As if seeing her distress, her mother sat beside her on the bed, covering her hand with her own. "But don't worry. Women like Cassandra and Leonie will just pop their babies out. It is delicate flowers like yourself who should worry. And one last piece of advice, my child—"

Willa didn't know if she wanted to hear it.

"—don't trust your husband. *Ever.* His only interests are his own and never yours. Remember to expect those little betrayals and you will have a decent marriage." She came to her feet. "Now, are you ready to leave for St. Stephen's?"

$\mathcal{C}hapter$ 5

$\mathcal{S}$t. Stephen Walbrook Church was one of the architect Christopher Wren's masterpieces. It was a marvel of stone Corinthian columns, dark wainscoting, and plasterwork. The dome over the altar was said to be Wren's original design for St. Paul's. The architect had been the genius behind rebuilding both churches after the Great Fire. The sunlight from a fine autumn day poured in through high windows that mimicked the arch of the dome and caught on the dust motes in the air scented with hint of holy incense.

It was a good place to marry and Matt was pleased. Indeed, he was now firmly convinced this marriage was a grand idea.

An acolyte was lighting candles around the altar. Close by, Soren, Lord Dewsberry, spoke to a man to who appeared to be the minister. Matt had not doubted that Soren would be here. He'd known he could count on him. Cassandra sat in the front pew on the left side. She waved at Matt.

With Minerva on his arm, Matt walked toward his friend. "What is Lord Dewsberry doing here?" his grandmother asked in a low undertone.

"He is to be my groomsman."

Minerva dug her heels. "Your groomsman? He can't be. Your groomsman should be a bachelor. Everyone knows that."

"I don't know any bachelors—"

"Of course you do," Minerva snapped. She had turned so that her back was to Soren, who had started toward them. He had taken Cassandra's arm to come greet him, with the minister following in their steps. The small party wisely stopped when they sensed trouble. "You have cousins who are bachelors and fitting for the role," Minerva said.

"—whom I trust," Matt finished, praying Soren couldn't overhear them. "Dewsberry is my choice. He's a man I can count on."

"He's married. This is in defiance of all the rules."

"Grandmother," Matt chided, wanting her to cease harping, "who are we to worry about rules? I am Camberly."

"That doesn't mean you can defy tradition. You are most fortunate I thought to procure a ring because you hadn't made any plans . . ." Her voice trailed off. She looked past him. Matt heard soft steps on the stone floor.

He turned, expecting to see his bride and her parents. Instead, his two oldest sisters, Alice and Kate, entered the sanctuary.

Matt raced to them. They were dressed in their best, heavy muslins with patterns on the fabric and fringed shawls. They had decorated their bonnets themselves. He knew because as a lad he'd watched them gathered around a table sewing on bows, fabric, and pheasant feathers.

All his sisters were tall, with Kate being the tallest. She was an actress, as their mother had been. She was a year younger than Alice. They were both bold and lovely women. Alice's soft brown hair had streaks of gray, but Kate's was still as black as when she was twenty. Matt was certain Kate knew a trick or two to keep herself young and would use them. Whereas Alice didn't worry about such things.

Kate had founded a small traveling theater company, quite a challenge for a woman alone. She was still single and doted on her nieces and nephews, as had Matt until the title had drawn him away.

The moment he reached them, Matt spread his arms wide and

gave them both a hug. He'd not seen them since well before their grandfather's death. They had not been invited to the funeral. But he had specifically ordered they receive an invitation to his wedding. He'd done at least that much.

"I'm so glad you are here," he said. "It's been too long."

"We had to see our brother marry," Alice said, righting her bonnet, which Matt's hug had knocked to one side. "Although I will tell you Roland has his hands full with the shop and the children." Alice and her husband were chemists in Cambridge.

"Besides," Kate said, "the family needs to look over this woman you are bringing into it." Her eyes went over to their grandmother, who still stood right where Matt had left her, quite obviously looking down her nose at his sisters. "You know how we *abhor* riffraff," Kate finished, indicating the dowager with a tilt of her head.

"I'm sorry, Kate," Matt said. It was all he could say. Henry and Minerva's disapproval was a heavy weight. He knew. Even though they had reluctantly supported his education after his parents' deaths, and with Alice's prodding, they had made him feel unworthy of their concern. That is, until William's death. Once Matt became the heir, their attitudes had changed—but they had never extended any interest or concern toward his sisters.

"She is a troll," Kate said of their grandmother.

"Kate," Alice prodded.

"Do you have a better description?" Kate challenged her sister.

"I don't waste my time with resentment."

"I do. It keeps me happy," Kate answered.

Matt changed the subject. "Jenny and Amanda couldn't come?"

"They are both breeding," Kate said.

"The midwife believes Amanda is having twins," Alice informed him. "She swears she can hear two heartbeats. They are due in two months. She is miserable and is making Robert miserable as well." Robert was a Cambridge tutor. He'd been trying to help Matt find a place on the staff when his grandparents had called him to London.

"Jenny is at the beginning of her term, but you know she hates to leave Marlin, and they don't have the money for a trip to London."

"But I offered to pay for your trips," Matt said. "Even Marlin's and Roland's and the children. And I insisted that you stay with me. There is room for twenty in the London house."

His sisters exchanged a look, one that made him pause. "You received an invitation for the ceremony and the breakfast, didn't you? I instructed Minerva's secretary to be certain your names were added to the guest list. I told her to write and let you know that you were welcome under my roof." He realized even as he spoke that he should have done it himself. He'd given the order to Minerva's secretary because he'd not spared the funds to hire his own man of business . . . but letters to his sisters? *He* should have written those.

"Oh, my," Kate said, her eyes rounding with innocence as she saw that Matt was beginning to understand his request had been countermanded, "we were left off the list *again*." She scowled in Minerva's direction before confessing, "I read the announcement in the papers. I contacted the others."

"And you received *no* invitation?"

Alice shook her head.

Matt could have throttled his grandmother. But then, his sisters were his family. He'd failed them. "I'm sorry, I should have seen to the matter." Instead he'd buried himself away with hurt pride, self-pity, and frustration.

"It doesn't matter," Alice decreed, and then she straightened her shoulders. "Actually, we are here to ensure the dowager—"

"The troll," Kate corrected, liking the name for Minerva that she'd coined.

"—isn't forcing you into a disastrous match over money. Truly, Matt, I don't know how our grandfather could have lost a fortune, but I will not see your future sacrificed for their mistakes."

"How do you know about the state of my affairs?" Matt asked, his gaze narrowing.

"Everyone knows," Alice said gently. "Even out in the country."

"We also know that you're marrying for money, and that isn't right, Matt. It isn't," Kate insisted. She placed her hand on his arm. "In our family, we marry for love. Just as Mother and Father did. I could have married for money. There has been many a rich old codger who has wanted to climb my bones—"

"Keep your voice down. We are in church, Kate," Alice said.

"There isn't anything I could say here that hasn't been said from any pulpit," Kate answered. "And Matt's happiness is at stake." She picked up the threads of her point. "Father would be disappointed to know you are selling yourself for his outdated aristocratic family who can't manage their affairs."

"It is a bit more complicated than that, Kate," Matt said.

His sister rolled her eyes. "Please, Matthew, we know the old duke was foolish with his money. Remember the stories Father told about how the old duke would spend a fortune on a special mash for his horses but couldn't be bothered to buy seed for his cottagers when the crops failed, or support the village school?" She frowned, lifting a suspicious brow. "Or have you become that sort of duke? Are you taking care of your people?"

He held up a hand. He wasn't going to go into the tale of blackmail with Kate, or justify his actions to date. "I'm trying to do what is right. Hopefully it will be the right thing for all of you. I will soon be able to help pay for education for my nieces and nephews. I can help support your troupe, Kate—"

"I don't need help."

"As you say, but if you do, I'm there."

"Yes, like you have been ever since Henry and Minerva decided you were second best but will have to do," Kate fired back.

"They have always been that way," Matt answered. "However, I've held my own." That wasn't completely true.

"But are you also doing what is right for you?" Alice pressed. "Marriage is too hard to live it with a stranger."

"And love isn't all they claim it to be, either," Matt flashed back. He kept his voice low, drawing his sisters closer. "However, whatever you think, I have made my decision. Besides, love isn't some panacea for everything. It won't buy seed or pay for the village school. And I will tell you something else, I'm better off without it."

Because, he realized, he loved too deeply. That was what had happened between him and Letty. He could see it clearly now. This lore in his family that love reigned supreme had given him flawed expectations, expectations that had almost gutted him.

He was happy his wayward heart didn't feel love for his soon-to-be bride. There would be no more disappointments in his life—

The entrance door flew open and was caught by a liveried footman. Leland Reverly marched into the church with his customary swagger.

"Good morning, Your Grace," Reverly barked out heartily. "A great day for a wedding, isn't it?" His wife followed him. She was dressed in purple, a rich shade tinged with red and not at all like his grandmother's lavender gown, and yet, for some reason, Matt sensed she wore it for mourning. Certainly, her expression lacked her husband's satisfaction.

And then all conscious thought left Matt's mind, as Willa's petite figure followed her mother into the sanctuary. She had her head down as she tried to keep her skirts from brushing the door but then she looked up, and suddenly stopped at the sight of Matt.

A beautiful woman could capture any man's attention, but there was something unique and special beyond the mere physical about Willa.

Her hair was piled high on her head, with a few artless strands curling down to her shoulders. The dress was an ethereal white that brought a glow to her skin. Her dark blue eyes met his. Her lips parted, and he almost took a step forward, wanting to touch her to see if she was real.

He opened and closed his gloved fingers. She wore pearl-tipped pins in her hair. He had an urge to pull them from her curls and watch her hair tumble down around her.

And this night, *his* wedding night, he would.

Ever since his grandparents had plucked him out of the obscurity of being a lowly tutor, he'd made a muddle of things. But *here* was a new beginning. For the title, for his family, including all those unborn nieces and nephews . . . and for himself.

Behind him, he heard Kate say to Alice, "Well, apparently we didn't need to be concerned after all."

Chapter 6

A knot had settled in Willa's stomach.

Besides her unsettling earlier conversation with her mother, her father was behaving as if this day was all about his prestige and reputation. He'd spent the morning barking at the servants and criticizing her mother. He'd made it clear in the coach ride that he considered the marriage ceremony an annoyance.

"I hope the minister doesn't go on and on. The receiving line starts exactly at noon. I'll walk out of the church even before the vows if I must."

"The Reverend Beam knows of your concerns," her mother had answered, repeatedly.

Her father had still grumbled his answer, his toe tapping with irritation, as if urging the horse and coach to move faster.

Willa's cousin Janie was with them. She had agreed to serve as Willa's bridesmaid. She was three years younger and very nervous, especially around Leland, who threw his weight around with his extended family.

The moment the coach had rolled up to the church door, he had charged ahead, leaving Willa and her mother to the footmen. He'd even ignored the small crowd of well-wishers and oglers who had gathered in front of the church because they'd heard there was to be a wedding of "important people."

Fortunately, they were more interested in Willa than in her father. She'd given them a small wave.

"Ignore them," her mother had ordered.

"They can do no harm."

"Really, you are to be duchess," her mother answered. "Act like one." With those words, she'd gone into the church.

"What shall we do?" Janie had whispered. She held a small bouquet of hothouse roses and asters that Willa was to carry.

"Follow her," Willa answered. She had offered one last wave and then had stepped out of the sun into the St. Stephen's sanctuary. She'd been in and out of this church most of her life; however, she was caught off guard at the sight of Matt standing not more than ten feet from the front door.

She hadn't known where she'd thought he would be. Of course, over the past weeks, she'd been more concerned about whether he would make an appearance at the ceremony than she had been about other details.

And now, here he was, looking tall and more handsome than any male of her acquaintance.

He was the very image of a noble. He wore full dress for the occasion of their wedding. His coat was a deep blue, the color of the night sky, over white breeches and hose. His waistcoat was gold embroidered silk.

She caught a scent of his shaving soap. It reminded her of the woods.

A sense of calm fell upon her. The knot in her stomach vanished.

Her father had gone past Matt to have a word with Reverend Beam, presumably to make more threats about walking out if the cleric didn't hustle the vows along. Her mother sent him an exasperated look, but Matt was focused on her.

He walked toward her, his blue eyes intent.

Did a bride curtsey to her husband?

Before she could riddle out the question, Matt took her gloved hand. "You look beautiful," he said, sounding as if they were a love match and not the arranged marriage all the world knew.

She felt herself flush, and he reached up and touched her heated cheek with the back of his gloved fingers. "Nervous?"

Willa nodded.

"I confess I am as well. But don't be afraid, we will do well together, Willa."

That was the promise she had needed to hear. And it gave her a very bad case of what must certainly be Annie's "tingles."

He pulled her forward. "Please, meet my sisters. This is Mrs. Alice Potter and Miss Kate Addison." To his sisters, he said, "I'm marrying well, aren't I?"

Kate lifted an eyebrow, an expression Willa had seen cross Matt's face a few times just in the short period she had known him. Kate was going to withhold judgment, but Alice was not as reserved.

She offered her hand to Willa. "Miss Reverly, I pray you and my brother are very happy."

"Please call me Willa. I don't believe we should stand on ceremony among family."

That statement earned her a nod of approval from Kate, who offered her own hand. Matt's sisters were very tall. "I hope you beat him daily," Kate said.

Willa's lips parted in shocked surprise. Kate was audacious, and Willa adored her. She smiled at the older woman. "I shall try," she promised, "although unless he waits while I fetch a stepstool, it may be difficult."

Kate laughed, the sound very much like her brother's. "Wait until he is asleep," she advised. "It is easier when they are prone."

"She does not need your advice, Kate," Matt said, taking Willa's arm and leading her up the aisle toward the altar.

"Knowing the shortcuts is important," Kate answered sanguinely from behind them.

Looking over her shoulder, Willa promised, "We shall talk later." This time even Matt laughed, and that was when Willa spied Janie still by the door. Her cousin acted like a nervous mouse afraid to take a step in. "Wait," she asked Matt. He stopped.

"Janie, please join us," Willa said.

Her cousin scurried up the aisle as if she feared she'd blundered at her duties. Willa tried to reassure her. "Thank you for my bouquet," she said, and then made introductions. "Your Grace, this is my cousin Miss Wright."

Janie curtseyed, her action so abrupt, she dropped the bouquet. Matt was gallant enough to pick it up. "Thank you for helping us with our wedding," he said, and Willa feared poor Janie would swoon.

Cassandra came forward and stepped into the fray, offering Willa a hug and gaining an introduction to Janie. Cassandra then smartly shepherded the poor girl toward the altar where the ceremony would be performed.

Matt had seen to seating the dowager in the front pew. She scowled at his sisters, who wisely chose to sit a pew behind and across the aisle from their grandmother, right behind Willa's parents. Willa wondered what they had done to offend the dowager.

"Time is passing," her father announced in a booming voice that echoed off the church's stone columns.

"Yes, we must be on with it," Matt agreed, and without ceremony, offered his arm to lead Willa to the altar.

The church fell quiet as the ceremony began. Willa was a bit surprised that Soren was her husband's groomsman. Cassandra had said nothing of it the day before.

Of course, when they spoke, the question had been *if* there would be a marriage sacrament, not who would be in attendance.

Matt said his vows in a clear, deep, confident voice.

When repeating hers, Willa started at a whisper. Her mother's disturbing words echoed in her head, especially now that she was standing before an altar. Off to the side, she heard her father snort his impatience.

She focused on Matt, meeting his eye. He smiled patiently. Her voice picked up strength.

It was true she barely knew her husband. Rumors surrounded him, but he also had sisters who obviously cared for him.

She'd listened to him vow to protect, love, and comfort her. He'd promised to forsake all others and be faithful.

In this space of time, she wished to believe him, and used her vows as a way to reassure herself.

Matt surprised her with a wedding band of scrolled gold set with tiny emeralds. After the ring had been blessed, he slipped it on her finger. It fit perfectly and was completely to her tastes.

In that moment, Willa's heart began to open.

Months of doubt evaporated.

He'd promised they would be good together. She now let herself believe him. Her fingers closed around his.

Matt noticed the gesture. He smiled, tightened his hold, and she couldn't help but grin like a daffy fool.

Yes, he was almost too handsome to be mortal. There would always be women eyeing him. However, he acted kind and she believed he was honest. The humiliation of being alone and having to wait for him no longer mattered. Instead, she chose to think about the future.

Reverend Beam held his hands high over their heads. In officious tones, he announced, "Now that Matthew Reginald Addison and Willa Louise Reverly have given themselves to each other by solemn vows, with the joining of hands and the giving and receiving of a ring, I pronounce that they are husband and wife, in the name of the Father, and of the Son, and of the Holy Spirit." He paused before finishing with great flourish, "Those whom God has joined together, let no one put asunder."

It was done. She was married. To the one man every woman in London wanted.

Including her.

"Good," her father said, clapping his hands and interrupting her savoring the realization of the moment. He came to his feet. "My daughter is a duchess. Your Grace, we will settle some details this afternoon." And then he proclaimed in more sonorous tones than those used by the priest, "To the House of Reverly-

Addison." He referred to the name Matt had agreed to take on as part of the marriage bargain. Reverly-Addison. It was a mouthful, and yet, Willa experienced a surge of pride. Her family would not disappear into history.

"But we must hurry along our way," her father said. "The guests will be arriving shortly. Your Grace?" He offered the dowager his arm, and in a blink, they were off toward the door, her mother trailing behind them.

"Janie, you will want to go with them," Willa said.

Her mother had heard the comment and stopped. "Yes, come, Janie. Your mother will be waiting at the house."

Janie acted relieved to be dismissed from her bridal duties.

"Willa is yours now, Camberly," her father cheerfully called as he started through the door a footman held open. "Have her at the house before noon."

Matt said he would happily, but then he took time to thank the clergy, passing a coin purse to Reverend Beam. It was a task Willa knew usually fell to the groomsman, but Matt had apparently chosen to perform it himself. She liked that. He wasn't one to conform to Society. He did as he thought right.

She believed it was original of him to have Soren, a married man, as his groomsman. She would have preferred Cassandra to have served as her bridesmaid instead of Janie. It would have made the ceremony more personal. But she'd lacked her husband's independence.

Cassandra gave her a huge hug. "Congratulations. You look beautiful, and I know you will be happy." She whispered for Willa's ears alone, "He will be good to you. He _will_."

Matt had turned to his sisters, who were waiting to offer their congratulations. "You are coming to the wedding breakfast." It was an order.

"We weren't invited. Please, Matt, don't make a fuss. We are fine," Alice said. "We'll just return to my friend Clara's house where we are staying."

"Please, celebrate with us," Willa said, adding her voice to her husband's—her first wifely duty. "My father is laying a table that could feed five thousand. Please, come."

It was Kate who decided it. "I'm going. If for no other reason than to stand behind the dowager's chair and make her acknowledge we are family." She pulled a face to demonstrate how she would look down on her grandmother while pretending to be some ferocious animal.

Alice and Matt laughed but Willa was confused, and then dared to say, "Her Grace acts as if you have offended her."

"The fact we breathe air offends her," Kate answered.

It was Matt who explained. "Our father was deemed the black sheep of the family for marrying beneath him. Grandmother goes to great lengths to remind my sisters that she considers them disowned."

"And yet, she dotes on you," Willa said.

"She hasn't always," Matt answered. "Still, she has treated me far better than she has them."

"It is because he is male," Kate said in an exaggerated whisper. "He has a rodney."

Rodney? And then Willa realized she was talking about his male bits. Her mouth started to drop, until she caught Kate observing her closely.

"An innocent, aren't you?" Kate said.

To such outspokenness? In a church? Yes, Willa was. However, she didn't want Kate to know. "It doesn't seem right to ignore all but one member of the family."

"It isn't," Kate agreed, somewhat cheerfully.

Alice said, "The old duke and his wife were very rigid in their views. Father defied them when he married Mother and they were furious. They claimed they could never forgive him . . . and then it became too late for a reconciliation. Our parents died of a fever."

"That is sad," Willa said. Cassandra nodded.

"It was Alice who forced our grandfather to do what was right for Matt," Kate said.

"And that is how I met him in school," Soren interjected. "His one and only friend. May I offer you two a ride in our vehicle? That way we can give our bride and groom a moment alone before they face the crush invited to celebrate their wedding."

"Thank you," Alice said.

"Well, then let us go. As groomsman, I need to shepherd everyone to the party." Soren spoke with the good humor Willa's father had lacked. "Reverend Beam, will you join us?"

"Is there room, my lord?"

"We shall squeeze you in," Soren assured him, and the minister agreed.

Matt offered Willa his arm, and the group of them left. Outside, the small crowd in front of the church had waited for them. There were a few cheers and then Matt swept Willa up into his arms to place her in the Camberly coach, a lumbering black vehicle with his ducal signet on the door. Their admirers liked the grand gesture and shouted their approval.

And Willa found herself happy. She finally allowed herself to be caught up in the heady rush of realizing this marriage was giving her a place in the world. Her husband was handsome; her friend Cassandra was near at hand; why, Matt even had sisters whom she rather liked and looked forward to knowing better.

Yes, the horses pulling the coach looked as if they were hired, and not from the best of stables. It didn't matter. Willa's dowry would give them all they needed. She could do that for him. And for his sisters, she realized. His whole family would benefit, even the dowager.

He climbed into the coach with her, his large body taking up most of the space. He rapped on the roof and they rolled forward.

For a second, they were quiet. Willa looked at her husband expectantly for a clue as to what they should do next.

He leaned back against the seat, setting his hat on the faded velvet cushion beside him. "Well, it is done," he said.

She nodded, suddenly shy.

"I'll be a good husband to you," he said.

His statement seemed odd to her. "I didn't think you wouldn't."

He reached out a hand. They had each given their gloves to their attendants and had not taken them back. She placed her left palm in his. His hand seemed very strong in comparison to hers.

She looked up at him and wished he would kiss her. Just as he had on her wrist, but on her lips. She was past ready for that first kiss.

Instead, he said, "I've been too caught up with other matters. I should have paid more attention."

Immediately, Willa thought of Letty Bainhurst. She didn't wish to, but that was where her mind went.

"There was so much to be done at Mayfield," he continued. "I know little of estate management and have had much to learn. I should have contacted my sisters. I feel selfish," he finished, obviously unaware of how his admission reassured Willa.

Her jealousy embarrassed her, especially coming on the heels of the vows she'd just made. The gold of her wedding band winked at her.

He was her husband now. He'd done all that was honorable. Matt was not her father. He wasn't.

And she wasn't her mother.

"I'm certain they understand."

"It doesn't excuse what I did." He released his breath as if coming to a decision. He looked at her. "But I'll be good from here on forward."

Once again, her heart seemed to expand a bit more in her chest. He was a good man. She'd married a good man.

The coach pulled up at the door of her house. Guests were already arriving. A queue had formed, and Peters, the butler, had the task of managing matters so that no one's sensibilities were insulted.

The coach door was opened. Matt leaped out first and then helped Willa to the ground.

Leland Reverly stood inside the door. "Take your places," he said impatiently. "Hurry."

Matt and Willa exchanged looks. Willa was thankful he was tolerant of her father.

The moment they were in their proper places in line and had put on the gloves they had retrieved from their attendants, her father nodded for Peters to shut the front door and then open it anew as if welcoming the world, and that was who seemed to arrive.

Guests poured through the door to be met with as much pomp and fanfare as her father could afford.

Willa knew many of the guests whether she'd talked to them or not. They flattered her and called her "Your Grace." Women curtseyed, and men bowed . . . women and men who would have barely given her any consideration only months ago.

Lady Wellington came through the line. "I see you took my advice to heart," she said to Willa. "Good for you."

"What advice?" Matt wished to know. He'd been having a few words of quiet conversation with his cousin George Addison, who had been introduced to Willa as a lawyer. She'd heard of him, of course. Her father knew him well.

Instead of answering, Lady Wellington merely smiled, tapping her fan against her cheek, and moved on down the line.

In truth, Willa could not have asked for a more attentive bridegroom than Matt. He was far more outgoing than she. He greeted people easily, presented her to those she did not know, and always included her in any conversations.

By the time her father called an end to the receiving line, Willa was starved. However, the serving was a bit tedious. There were so many people, service didn't end until almost three. Everyone had been fed but many were now seriously doing damage to the Reverly cellars. Her father was leading the pack. Even the dowager appeared more than a bit tipsy.

Because the celebration was so huge, guests filled several rooms. To her relief, Matt was sober. He circulated through the rooms with Willa in order to spend time with all their guests. She liked being by his side. She felt important.

At one point, Cassandra drew her close to whisper, "Do we still need to have the coach waiting to help you escape to Cornwall?"

Willa glanced over to where Matt was involved in conversation with Soren and another gentleman. Of the group, her husband was easily the most handsome. She linked her arm with Cassandra's and led her to an alcove. "No," she answered. "I believe I'm well pleased. However, I must talk to you."

"What is it?"

There were people all around them and barely a private place to be had, but Willa needed to ask the questions that had been burning in her mind ever since her mother's conversation that morning. Bringing her lips almost to Cassandra's ear lest she be overheard, she said, "Mother fears that the marriage bed might be difficult for me."

Cassandra's eyes widened. "What did she say to you? You've gone pale."

"She fears for me because my husband is a big man and I'm so petite."

Cassandra took her hand. "Willa, it will be fine. Matt is a good man. He won't hurt you. Don't worry about it."

"Was it painful for you?"

"No. And I count the hours in my husband's arms, in that bed, the best part of the day. Besides, didn't Lady Bainhurst claim he was the best of lovers? If anyone can reliably rate lovers, it is Letty. That is all the women at the tables can talk about."

"At *my* wedding feast? That is outrageous."

"Well, not if it is true. Oh, come, Willa, it is not a bad thing to marry a man who knows what he is about. As to the fact that he is tall and you are much smaller, I've met other odd couples in height. They never act as if it is a problem."

Her words relieved Willa. "Thank you."

Cassandra gave her a hug. "I want you to be happy. You deserve it. We all do. And after I have this baby, you and I will travel to see Leonie. Doesn't that sound like the best idea?"

"It does. Let's plan on it."

A maid approached Willa. "Excuse me, Your Grace, but your mother asks you to join her at her table."

"Don't listen to wives' tales," Cassandra warned, and Willa nodded before following the maid. She looked to see where her husband was and discovered that he was involved with a group of men. However, from another doorway, her mother was signaling she wished Willa's presence. Willa soon found herself making small talk to her mother's card friends.

As soon as she was able, Willa excused herself and went in search of her husband.

The crowd was growing seriously unruly, their tongues loosened by free-flowing spirits. If Willa had been in control of this event, the servants would be gathering glasses by now. However, her father liked this sort of madcap affair.

One man, her father's age, charged up to her, demanding to kiss the bride. He started to take advantage of Willa's size by trying to pick her up and give her a sloppy kiss. She was quite adept at dodging such silliness. Spirits made everyone forget themselves and she had no desire to make a scene. She slipped from his arms and moved out into the hall.

The guest shouted for her to come back and the other people in the room shouted for him to sit down, some even pulling him into a chair.

Willa needed air. Or to pull the pins out of her hair.

The back rooms of the house were quieter. She moved to the garden door that had been propped open to take advantage of the lovely day, but then stopped when she heard her husband talking to Kate.

She would have announced herself except she heard Kate say, "Willa *is* lovely. And I'm certain she will make an impeccable duchess even if she is little more than a child herself."

That was a statement to stop Willa in her steps.

"Stop it, Kate. Willa is a woman in every way."

"She's an example of the pampered class. She knows little of the world. And her eyes follow you everywhere as if you are some treasure someone has placed in her lap."

Did she have that expression? Willa didn't think so . . . except she could admit to being slightly dazzled by her husband's good looks.

She was pleased that her husband defended her. "She is far stronger and more sensible than you imagine," he assured his sister.

"I'm certain you are right. However, in our family, we marry for *love*, Matt. We learned that from our parents."

"There is the title—" he started, but she cut him off.

"*Love*. That's all that is important. Why do you think I am still single? I refuse to settle for anything less. So, tell me you love Willa and I shall shut my mouth. Even after your ridiculous decision to join her name to yours."

"Kate." He said her name as if wishing she would understand.

"Matt." She mimicked his tone, unrelenting in her demand.

He made an impatient sound and then said, "Our parents were fortunate. What they had was rare. I've seen it in no one else—"

"Alice and Roland, Amanda and Robert—" Kate began ticking off.

Matt interrupted her. "I know, I know. They are all lucky, because I will tell you, I've been in love. Yes, see, you didn't know that, Kate. It made a bloody fool of me. No, worse, it almost destroyed me. This is better. I respect Willa."

"And her sizable dowry," Kate added, sounding disenchanted. "How touching."

"That will see this family through difficult times," Matt assured her.

"Do you think money is what we want from you? That it is the reason Alice and I traveled to London? If you do, then I pity Willa. Marriage is hard, Matt. Without love, it is little more than a business transaction."

"Says someone who has never been married or in love."

There was a pause as if his words had struck home. And then she said, "I don't understand how you went so far astray. There must be a reason, and I'll wager the fault lies with *you*." She must have walked off with those words because he tried to call her back.

Willa wished she'd never heard this conversation.

Of course, she and Matt were not a love match. All she'd asked was to be respected and to be valued.

But he'd also said he'd loved someone else . . .

Willa knew who.

She had no reason for jealousy, and yet, every time Letty's name was mentioned, acid soured her stomach. It had been this way since the night of their betrothal when he'd left London without a thought of Willa. And now was he merely placating her?

She had a strong urge to start upending tables and throwing glassware—which was very out of character for her.

Instead, she found a quiet corner and sat because she was always polite. Well bred. Raised to be a duchess. Even if she was as blank and boring as the pieces of paper on her desk yesterday.

And, really, what should she have expected? Matt's poems might have inspired an almost desperate hope in her for something meaningful between them, but now she realized they were nothing but words.

She thought about her father's mistresses. The humiliations her mother was forced to live with because she was dependent upon her husband's whims, his moods. All any woman did was sell herself into marriage. What other option was there for them?

"Here you are," Matt's voice said from behind her. He came walking from the front of the house. No one's smile was better than his. If she let herself, she could imagine he was happy to see her.

But Kate was right. They did not know each other.

He was a stranger.

He offered his arm. "It is time for us to go. This group is growing rowdier and I want you to myself." There was a warmth to his tone. He sounded as if he meant the words.

For the briefest of seconds, Willa held back, stuck by how much she wanted to believe he had feelings for her, until she realized it was useless. This man was her husband. Her father had paid money to him. Reverly-Addison.

Like it or not, he was her fate. The best her life would be.

"Yes, please, let us go." She tried to sound bright.

After all, it was her wedding day. She was expected to be happy.

And Willa always played her role well. She knew how to smile, when what she truly wanted to do was scream.

Chapter 7

$\mathcal{M}$att was furious with Kate.

How dare she blacken his wedding day with her accusations. She always thought she knew better, that she had not only a right, but an obligation to voice her opinion. Thank God, his other sisters were more discreet.

However, now that she'd pricked his conscience, he wanted to prove her wrong.

He had no doubt that she would report to his other sisters that poor Matt had lost his way. That he wasn't the man he should be.

Well, he was damn tired of families all the way around.

It was true he was marrying Willa to save the impossible situation he had inherited. No, he wasn't completely happy with the solution. He'd been resigned to being a lowly tutor. However, fate had conspired otherwise and given him the responsibility to preserve what his ancestors had built. He owed his descendants his very best.

Yes, he would have preferred to have had the luxury of marrying for love. Damn it all, he'd been so inspired by his parents' example, he'd written a book of poetry about it. A bad book, but a book all the same. He believed in love . . . or thought he did.

He had lost his way in his affair with Letty. Looking back, he realized it had been doomed to fail from the beginning. Bainhurst was so possessive, he would never have divorced Letty for criminal conversation. They would have had to run away to the Continent, and Matt now realized he would have eventually come to his senses and regretted sacrificing everything meaningful in his life for her.

In that respect, Letty had been far wiser than he.

Marrying Willa was the right thing to do, no matter what Kate said. The Reverly money allowed him to take care of his sisters, his grandmother, and the numerous cottagers and tenants that depended on his sensible management of Mayfield for their livelihood.

Not only all of that, he actually liked Willa. He didn't mind changing his last name to Reverly-Addison. Granted, Kate would have a field day if she knew how little time he had spent with Willa before the wedding.

Or that Willa hadn't sparked his interest until she'd been willing to cut him loose.

However, now the deed was done. And he'd be lying if he claimed it didn't feel good to have Willa's dowry. Overnight, she'd resolved the majority of his problems. He owed her his allegiance and, to his mind, so did Kate.

So he was determined to give Willa all the deference that was her due as he moved toward the front door with his new wife on his arm.

Numerous suggestions of how they were to spend their night were called out. A few were crass enough to make comment about the difference in their height. Throughout the afternoon, Matt had overheard people speculating. He'd quickly steered Willa away from that nonsense.

In truth, he didn't know if she was sensitive about her height or understood how men viewed women as playthings. A group of men had mentioned that he was fortunate to have such a doll-like wife, the lust in their voices enough to make Matt contemplate throwing them out the door.

Soren had calmed him down. "It's the brandy," he'd said. "People are damn fools."

Matt could agree to that.

The worst, though, had happened after Matt had finished with Kate. He had searched for Minerva to let her know he was planning on leaving and caught her holding court with her friends on whether a woman as petite as Willa could give birth to a child sired by a man as big as he was.

"Big babies have difficulties coming out of small wombs," one of the dowager's friends had opined. "I had a maid die in childbirth for that very reason. Both she and the baby dead. Couldn't get it out of her."

Talk of wombs was not a deterrent to a man with sisters as vocal as the ones Matt had. The idea that his children would die made his brain spin.

Matt's first reaction was to denounce their speculation as nonsense. But what if it wasn't?

One of the few bits he'd learned about animal husbandry over his months at Mayfield was that breeders took great care in matching their males and females. However, those rules were about sheep, horses, and dogs.

Not people.

In fact, a good number of the women at the breakfast were as petite as Willa. Of course, none of their husbands were Matt's size.

He'd looked around for Alice, the scientific one, and found her deep in conversation with Kate. No, he wasn't going there.

Instead, he hunted for his wife. She'd been sitting on a chair in what seemed to be the one quiet corner of the house. She'd acted more than ready to leave.

Now they said their last good-byes as if embarking on a great trip and not just driving a few blocks to his house to consummate their union. Kate and Alice offered their well wishes; Kate with a decided lack of sincerity. He noticed that Willa's earlier warmth toward his outspoken sister had given away to a reserve. She saved her smile for Alice.

Minerva waved them on and returned to her friends. No one knew where Leland Reverly was, and his wife barely looked up from the card game she had started.

There were true well-wishers such as George and Cassandra and Soren. Matt chose to focus on them.

However, he was grateful once the coach door had closed.

He looked to Willa. "I'm glad that is over."

She studied some point out the window and nodded. The coach rolled forward. He found himself watching her, fascinated by her skin. The late afternoon sun highlighted its clarity.

His wife. He was not displeased. She still wore the virginal lace and net veil.

He removed his glove and reached out to run the backs of his fingers against her cheek.

Willa jumped at the contact. She looked to his hand and then at him. For once, he could read her thoughts in her eyes. "I didn't mean to frighten you," he said.

"I was startled. That is all." Her lashes lowered as she moved her study to her hands in her lap. "I'm tired. The day has been exhausting."

Matt could agree, except he was far from tired. All his senses were tuned to her.

Willa was a study in contrasts. She could be bold and then remarkably shy, submissive even. That was interesting because his experience had been that women, like men, were either one way or the other. They either forged ahead or held back. Willa could be a chameleon, unless one looked deeper.

He shifted in his seat, and again she jumped slightly—only this time, he sensed a hint of what she was thinking: his lady was angry.

Furious even.

That was why he couldn't decipher the expression in her eyes, because what man would expect an angry wife on his wedding day? Of all of life's days, this should be the one when the female was happiest.

"You are upset?" he said.

"Just tired," she answered.

He didn't believe her. "Have I done something to offend you?" he asked.

Willa looked at him wildly as if he'd spouted gibberish . . . or read her mind. "Of course not."

She was lying.

He let silence spool between them.

"Why would you even think such a thing?" she threw out. A shiver of distaste went through her as if the fault was his.

"Well," Matt said, "your whole attitude tells me you would rather be anywhere but right here."

She scrunched her nose. She'd never done that around him before. He liked it because he sensed it was something she tried not to do, and yet, it was charming. A personal quirk. She then brushed at an imaginary piece of lint on her skirt before saying, "We aren't a love match."

"True . . ." He would not deny it. "But that doesn't mean we can't *make love.*" He let his voice warm the last words and watched her reaction.

Willa fidgeted with her skirt, right where the imaginary lint had been. She rubbed her thumb against it as if there was a stain only she could see.

She was nervous. The idea struck like lightning. *God, he was a fool.* He'd thought she was angry. He'd actually been ready to take offense, but now he realized, she was shy. Yes, that was it. Maidens were shy . . . because they didn't know what to expect.

Matt had never slept with a virgin. He knew what the *ton* whispered about his carnal adventures, but a good deal of that had to do with Letty. In truth, he'd actually not had many sexual partners. Meaningless relationships had never been attractive to him.

However, Willa was *very* attractive, and she always had been. From their first introduction, he'd admired her English beauty and the way she held herself. He would never have agreed to marry her if he hadn't been somewhat drawn to her.

He leaned in, reaching for her hand rubbing the material and covered it with his own. His action brought his eyes level with hers. "I'm pleased with my choice of wife," he said, thinking that was important to say. "I won't hurt you, Willa. I promised we would be good together."

The corners of her mouth tightened.

He held his breath, waiting for her response and uncertain if he'd made the situation better or worse.

And then she leaned forward and pressed her lips against his.

The startling kiss was innocent, untried—and set a fire alight inside him.

Matt had not anticipated such a response to her artless inexperience. All admonishments to himself about maidens aside, he would have taken that kiss and more, if the coach had not come to a halt.

Willa broke the chaste kiss, her color high, a second before Marshall, the Camberly butler, opened the coach door himself. "Your Grace," he said to Willa with great flourish, "*welcome.*"

"Thank you," she managed, and offered Marshall her hand to help her out of the coach. Matt followed.

The servants were in a line by the front door. Willa hung back as if intimidated, but with a slight press of the fingers, Matt teased her forward. She went by every servant acknowledging their bows and curtseys of welcome. Fortunately, Matt didn't have even a third of the servants her father's household boasted or else they would be at it all day.

And this was not how he wanted to spend his time. He was ready to open a school for kisses and he had only one pupil in his mind: his sweetly innocent wife.

Inside, Mrs. Snow, the housekeeper, waited by the stairs to be introduced to the new duchess. "If you have any questions, Your Grace, I am completely at your service."

"That is nice—" Willa started, but Matt had waited long enough.

"Very nice," he agreed brusquely, a beat before sweeping Willa up in his arms, just as he had in front of the church. His arms full of wife, Matt looked to Marshall and Mrs. Snow. "Don't disturb us."

His pronouncement was met with good-humored laughter as he carried Willa up the stairs to his room.

Another servant waited for them there, Willa's maid. It had been arranged that while the wedding breakfast was taking place, Willa's clothing and personal effects would be moved to his house.

Her maid made a deep curtsey as they came upon her. "Annie," Willa said, "did the move go well?"

"Oh, yes, Your Grace, very well."

"Annie," Matt said, testing the name. "Your services will not be needed for the night." A grin of delight spread across her Irish face, and Matt decided he liked this new addition to his household. "Have a good evening," he tossed over his shoulder as he carried Willa into his bedroom. He kicked the door shut and conveyed her to his massive bed with the intention of pursuing that kiss they had started.

He was hard, he was ready . . . he was excited. If she'd been more experienced, Matt would already have her on her back. Instead, he remembered she'd been gently reared. Protected and pampered. Guarded.

And he'd taken a marriage vow to cherish her, one he was determined to obey if it killed him.

He removed his jacket.

THE TIME HAD come.

The moment everyone had gossiped about. Willa was going to let Camberly have her because he was her husband. Giving in to him was her duty. She wasn't truly his duchess unless they did the deed.

She experienced a pang of regret that she'd overheard his words to his sister about not loving her. Willa was practical. In spite of the marriage vows, she wouldn't even have thought of love if it hadn't been for Kate's words.

Now, it seemed all she could think about. *Love.*

Having a husband who loved *her.* Just as Soren loved Cassandra, and Leonie's husband, Rochdale, all but worshipped her.

And yet, everyone envied Willa. Matt was a prize. She had become a duchess. The point game had gone to her.

So why did she feel sad?

It might have to do with the kiss in the coach. Her first kiss. She hadn't known what she was about, but he had apparently liked it because he hadn't stopped touching her since she'd kissed him. For most of the afternoon, when she had been with him, his hand had been at her arm or her waist, guiding her and moving her along until he'd swept her up and carried her to his bed.

Willa sat up on the mattress. His bedroom furnishings were dark brown against ivory walls. The bed itself had been made for a giant. It had a massive headboard that was almost black with age. The bedclothes were a dull gold. Someone, most likely Annie or Matt's valet, had turned down the covers.

Rather bravely, she said, "What do you want me to do?"

He'd tossed his jacket onto a nearby chair and was tugging on the knot in his neck cloth when her question gave him pause. An uncertain look came into his eye, as if he, too, was feeling his way. And then he answered, "Let me take down your hair."

The request was unexpected—and she couldn't imagine anything she would more dearly love. The weight of it had added to her building anxieties. "Yes, please."

He smiled and pulled his neck cloth free to join his jacket before offering his hand. "Well then, stand." She thought he meant the floor until he helped her balance on the mattress. This way, she was taller than he was. He wasn't so intimidating this way. Was that his intent?

He began removing the pearl-tipped pins.

She held out her hand to receive them just as she did with Annie. The familiar arrangement helped her relax. "There are plain pins in there as well."

"I will find them." His touch was gentle, his expression intent. He reminded her of a sculptor she'd once observed working on his art. The tension between Willa's shoulders and neck began to unwind. "I've wanted to see your hair down since the moment we first met," he said.

"I have too much of it."

He smiled. "We shall see."

Her gaze took in the room. This was obviously his domain. Just as she noticed when she'd visited Mayfield several months ago, there were signs of neglect and wear. A huge wardrobe took up a good portion of one wall. There was a washstand, a desk, chairs—all the usual items in a bedroom, including a privacy screen in one corner.

However, Willa's personal effects were here. She was surprised. She had assumed she would have her own room. In fact, beyond his shaving gear, there seemed to be nothing else of Matt's in this room. What brushes and small boxes and bottles were on the washstand belonged to her.

He had collected all the pearl pins and was now searching for the plain ones.

"I was thinking this was your room," she said, "but my things are here."

"This is *our* room."

She looked down at him. "We'll share the same room?" She had never heard of such a thing. Her parents had separate suites of rooms.

"You are my wife, Willa. You sleep by my side."

"Forever?"

"As long as our natural lives." He pulled the last pin from her hair. It was as if that last pin held it all in place. Her hair tumbled down around her shoulders, flowing almost to her waist.

It was pure pleasure to have the weight of it off her neck. As she did every night when she took her hair down, she rotated her shoulders—and then stopped. Her breasts were at his eye level and they had his attention.

A warmth roiled deep in her lower belly and a curiosity in her mind.

His eyes had darkened with interest. He rested his hand on her waist. He raised his gaze to her. It was almost a sin for a man to have such dark lashes or such sparkling blue eyes.

"I want you, Willa. Do you understand exactly what that means?"

In this moment, it was as if they were the only two people in the world.

"I'm told to do what you tell me." Her mother's instruction didn't seem daunting at all right now. "And I will, although I don't know how good I will be at counting backward from a hundred."

If she had popped him in the nose, he couldn't appear more startled. "Count backward?"

Willa nodded, sinking down on the bed. She removed her kid slippers. It had bothered her to stand on the coverlet in them. "Mother suggested it. She said that way it will be all over before I know it."

Matt burst out laughing. He sat on the bed beside her as if it was the most natural thing in the world. "Count backward?"

Willa wasn't certain what was so funny. Should she not have told him? She nodded warily.

He caught her mood. "Please, I'm not laughing at you. I'm just . . ." He paused as if looking for a word and found it. "Charmed. I'm charmed to hear you say that. Your honesty, Willa, is a gift." He leaned back, resting on one arm, and gently pulled her with him. "You were told to count to a hundred?"

"Backward," Willa added. She caught her hair and pulled it over one shoulder so it wasn't beneath her.

His gaze met hers. He sobered. "My hope is that you are enjoying yourself so much, you can't remember how to count."

Her mother had not said anything about enjoyment. However, Cassandra had. "Is that why everyone claims you are a good lover?" An hour earlier she wouldn't have dared to say such a thing. However, being with him—like this—seemed completely right. Why, they both were still dressed.

"Now the pressure is on," he said in mock dismay followed by a self-deprecating smile. "That 'lover' gossip is stuff and nonsense. They prattle on like that because they have nothing else to talk about. The only opinion I am interested in is yours and, together, we'll find what pleases us both."

That was a very nice promise. Especially the word "together."

He stroked her hair, watching it flow through his fingers. "So lovely," he murmured before lifting his gaze to meet hers. "Willa, kiss me the way you did in the coach."

How could she refuse such a simple request?

Willa leaned toward him. Their lips met.

And she was kissing him.

It was a perfect kiss, or so she thought—until his lips parted and she felt his tongue trace the closed line of hers.

That tickled. Her startled lips parted and then he taught her something about kissing. Pressed lips had nothing over being able to drink the breath of her partner.

He didn't force. He waited until she moved toward him. The kiss took on a new life. Their mouths fit in a way she'd never imagined. With a soft sigh, Willa gave herself over to him because he knew more than she did, and she was liking the lesson. He drew her down to the bed, his arms gathering her close.

As if from a distance, she heard him slip off his shoes and let them drop to the hardwood floor. He eased her on her back so the kiss could deepen. She liked what he was doing with his tongue. She tried to copy his movements, catching his tongue and lightly stroking it with her own. He reacted by making their kiss fiercer, and Willa felt everything inside her rise toward him.

She *tingled*.

Every inch of her.

Just as Annie predicted.

It was Matt who broke it off. He was practically on top of her, but the weight of his body didn't bother her. In fact, like his kiss, it felt good.

He smiled down at her. His breathing had gotten heavy and she was conscious of their legs tangled together, their feet dangling off the edge of the bed. "I want to make love to you, Willa."

Love. There was that word again.

"But I will not do anything you don't like," he said.

She reached back and lifted her hair so that she wasn't lying on it. "I know you won't. I also believe you are right."

"About what?"

"The counting. I'm not going to bother because I don't want to be distracted. Not right now."

Camberly was handsome, that was true. But when he laughed, he was impossible to resist.

Before she knew what he was about, Matt rolled to his back, bringing her with him. She found herself astride his body, her bum on his abdomen. His hands pushed her skirts up to her thighs. She liked the feeling of him beneath her. He pulled the ribbons on her stockings, loosening them.

"The dress is beautiful on you, Willa. But I'd like to see you without it."

She'd known that husbands and wives were naked in bed together. However, she'd actually imagined that everything happened under covers and in the cloak of night.

Instead, the late day's sun came in through the room's many windows. She could hear the sounds in the house and on the street. No one knew what was happening in here save she and Matt . . . *her* husband.

Willa shook her hair back and dragged it forward out of her way. She reached behind her for the dress's lacing. His hands ran up and down her thighs. They were warm and knowledgeable. He began to unroll her stocking down her legs.

Where he touched, she grew heated.

She gathered her skirts, lifted them, and pulled her dress over her head. Of course, her hair caught in the material. Willa struggled until Matt rose to sit, moving her into his lap. He easily freed her.

Her thighs now cradled his hips. His lips pressed a kiss on her neck.

Willa didn't know what he did with the dress. She didn't care because he'd begun nibbling her skin, working his way up to her ear. She placed her hands on his shoulders. Her breasts were full and tight against her lawn chemise. She wore it and a thin petticoat tied at her waist and nothing more.

All the blood in her body, all the sensation, was flowing to a few key spots, including the juncture where she was snug against him.

She knew he was hard. No one could have missed that. Her body took his measure. Everyone's prediction was correct: he was not small.

But she was not afraid. Willa might not be certain of the mechanics, however she had a strong idea about what he was going to do—and she had never wanted something more in her life.

Her body began moving with an accord of its own as if anxious to be closer to him. She slid along his breeches, so sensitive she could feel every button and fold of clothing.

Matt bit her ear. The nip was a pleasure. She pressed herself down harder on him. He groaned, meeting her eye.

"You are perfect," he whispered. "The things you are doing to me."

He sounded as if she had power, as if she had control. "I think you are perfect, too."

His smile turned seductive. His hand hooked under the strap of her chemise. Her nipples were like hard buds. Usually she was embarrassed when they tightened, but not now. She let her shoulder slip out of the strap. He pulled it down, revealing her breast. He weighed it, stroked it, and then put his hot mouth against her, and Willa was undone.

Her hand pulled on the tapes of her petticoat, loosening it. She wanted him to touch all of her. Every inch of her body seemed to weep for his hand upon her.

Matt undressed her until she was sitting on his lap naked. He kissed her in places she'd not thought to be kissed. His hands ran over the indent of her waist and the curve of her hips.

She wanted him to never stop. But he did. He rested his palm against her belly, his fingers lowering to the most intimate part of her.

He touched her.

Willa gave a small cry at the exquisite, keen sensation.

He drew back and she followed him. "Is this it, Matt? Is this making love?" She felt as if drugged, as if only he knew what she needed.

"I didn't hurt you?"

"Lord, no."

"Shall I go on?"

He was still dressed, and yet, she did not mind. She rather liked it. She felt no shame even as she nuzzled his neck and whispered, "Please."

Matt touched her again, this time circling the tight nub. She leaned into him, savoring the smell of him, his strength, and the magic of his fingers. Her body was prepared for him. She opened herself wider, letting him have all he wanted, and he took full advantage by slipping two fingers inside her.

Willa paused. She wasn't certain. His lips brushed her ear. "It is all right." She believed him, and relaxed.

The strangeness of it left her. Her body eased around him. He began teasing her again, rubbing his thumb against that sensitive flesh while leaving his fingers right where they were. "Is that all right, Willa?" he'd asked in between kissing her forehead, her nose, her cheek, and then her mouth.

Oh, yes, it was.

Heat built inside her. She caught her breath. Her hands slid around his shoulders and then she wrapped her arms around his neck.

He grounded her even as he drove her in a direction she didn't quite comprehend—until she was *there*.

Her body understood. There was a tightening and then the most remarkable sense of well-being rippled through her in waves. It was as if she'd been holding herself as tight as a bowstring, only to discover the true pleasure was in letting go. She marveled at how agreeably pleasing it was.

Willa rested her head on his shoulder, savoring the enjoyment.

Matt captured her face, cupping it with both of his hands and turning her up to him. "You are amazing," he whispered. "Incredible."

He'd liked it as well.

Her hand ran over his shirt. "No, *you* are amazing." She sounded tipsy. She also realized why his smile was so devilish. He had a dimple. It was only on one side of his mouth and didn't appear often, but when it did, she had no defense against it.

Especially when he followed it with a kiss that curled her toes.

"I told you we'd be good together," he said. He moved her from his lap and pulled back the bedclothes. "Here, love."

She moved her unwieldy hair again to one side and slid under the sheets as he unbuttoned his waistcoat. She felt peaceful and drowsy. It had been a full day. A glass of wine would have been nice.

However, her senses perked up as Matt unbuttoned and took off the vest. He placed it on a chair close to the bed. He tugged his shirt over his head.

Willa couldn't help but stare. He'd seen all of her and she was most anxious to see all of him. Her observation that he had never needed padding in his jackets was quickly confirmed. His chest was hard lean lines. He wasn't a beefy man but sleek and smooth.

"You are staring," Matt said.

"Of course," she answered, and blushed at her own audacity.

"It is all right, Willa. Admire me all you will." With those words, he began unbuttoning his breeches.

Willa should look away.

She didn't.

Of course, she'd seen men's parts when she'd visited museums with Cassandra—but this was different. In marble or oil, the men's parts in art appeared to look like oysters without the shell. Their bits hadn't been appealing to her at all. She'd once said as much to Leonie and Cassandra and they had agreed.

Matt didn't look anything like an oyster. Rodney, Kate had said. His did look like a *rod*-ney. It was a staff with a knobbed head. A large one.

He folded his breeches and put them on the chair with his other clothes before climbing into the bed with her. He pulled the sheet over them.

"Are you all right?" he asked.

Willa wondered if she looked pale. She nodded. Then she had to ask, "Are they all that big?"

Matt knew exactly what she was asking about. "Yes," he answered. "Mine is actually quite normal."

However, it was bigger than two fingers. It was also very unattractive. Not as ugly as oysters, but not visually appealing, either.

"They are *all* like that?"

"Yes, Willa." He propped his head on one hand and said, "Are you all right?"

"You keep asking me that."

"I don't want you to feel as if I will overrun your wishes. Or that I am pushing you."

Understanding dawned on her. "We haven't coupled yet."

"No, we haven't. We were just enjoying each other."

She considered a moment. "Do I need to start counting now?"

He laughed and pulled her close to him. "I prefer you to kiss me instead."

That she could do.

It did not take many kisses before a deep yearning started building inside her again. It was as if he'd discovered what she liked best and this time, he'd set right to it.

She, too, had explored and learned a few things. Matt responded every time she kissed his ear. He adored her breasts and they felt very much the same way toward him in return.

And what she truly liked was his weight upon her.

His kisses became more purposeful. She began to realize how much he'd held himself back earlier. Now, it was as if he was being driven. As if she had unharnessed a force within him. His hands cupped her buttocks and curved her to him. The hair of his legs tickled her thighs as she cradled him. She pressed her breasts against his hard chest, her abdomen alongside his. In bed, their difference in height did not matter and she was soon willing to do whatever he wanted—

The tip of him pushed against her intimately. He stroked her with that very hard staff, mimicking the earlier strokes of his fingers. She flinched at the touch. He gentled her with soft words in her ear.

"Precious," he whispered. "So precious."

He meant her. She was what was "precious" to him.

Her legs opened to him. He felt good as he slid himself up and back. Very good.

Matt raised his weight up. He looked down at her, his eyes dark with concern, or was it lust? "This may hurt."

She had no fear. There had been some discomfort the last time, but pleasure had quickly replaced pain.

"I'll do this quick. You are so ready, but, Willa, I don't know if I can hold back once I start. Do you understand?"

She cupped his face in her hands. Looking into his eyes, she promised, "I will be fine."

His lips found hers. He kissed her, deep and hard. She curved toward him. She knew he would never hurt her.

The tip of the shaft was right where his fingers had been.

And then he thrust forward, and it *was* as if she was being rendered in two. A sheering pain cut through her.

Chapter 8

*M*att felt her tear.

He knew he should pause, to take a moment, but Willa had him. She was tight and closed around him. He'd never experienced anything that felt this good, this right.

His mind was not his own.

He registered her distress. His kiss swallowed her cry. Her hands moved from around his neck to pressing her palms against his shoulders. She tried to buck against him, to free herself, and that was not helping matters. It just drove him deeper—which was where he wanted to be, embedded in her.

Matt held still. What had started as exciting and lusty had turned dark and punitive. He also knew he couldn't let Willa go, not at this moment. She needed to understand what lay beyond the pain. That this joining was more than an animal act. There was beauty to it and deep satisfaction.

But first came pain.

It took all his stamina to hold himself steady. "Willa, Willa."

"Let me go."

"If I do, you'll never know. I don't want to hurt you. I don't." And yet, he knew he was. The joy was gone for her.

And for him.

Seconds seemed like hours until, at last, Matt did what he knew he must. He pulled out of her.

He acted against his every primitive impulse. As if in defiance, his seed released, but he had done as she demanded.

Willa turned her head from him. She stared at the far wall. She would not thank him for the strength of will he had exerted over himself. She was done with him.

Moving to one side, he fell upon the bed, one arm across her chest. He could not move.

And then she coldly shoved his arm away.

With energy he did not have, he made himself rise up. "Willa—"

She gave her back to him. He reached for her but she swatted him away, drawing her knees up. "You hurt me."

"It won't be like that next time."

"There won't be a next time." She pulled the covers around her. "I hated that." Her shoulders shook, and he realized she was crying.

"Willa, please. You tore. It had to have been painful—"

She shot him a wild look as if he was a murderer. "The whole thing is disgusting. I feel dirty and used. It is *foul*."

Her voice had risen, and Matt feared she was in danger of growing hysterical. How was it that he, a man who enjoyed sex, who worked to be a good lover and please his companions, had botched the whole matter with his wife?

He looked at his spent sex. It was already stirring again. The bastard had a mind of its own.

Matt reached to put his hand on her shoulder but then thought differently. She cried silently and it broke his heart. This was a woman who was accomplished at protecting her feelings. If she'd been one of his sisters, she would be tearing the room apart. Or him.

Instead, Willa dove deeper into her despair. It worried him.

"Willa, let me fetch you something to drink." A brandy would help steady her nerves.

She didn't respond so he acted. Rising from the bed, he found himself covered with her blood. He poured water in the basin and quickly cleaned himself before pulling on his breeches and his shirt. He went to the door.

Earlier, he'd given Marshall instructions on preparing a meal to be delivered to his room. A maid waited in the hallway for the sign.

Matt found himself praying that the walls were thick enough that she hadn't heard a sound from the bedroom. Fortunately, she was tactfully stationed far enough away that possibly she hadn't.

At the sight of him, she came to attention. He motioned for the food and mouthed, "Bring brandy." She nodded her understanding and was off.

He closed the door. The day's light was fading. Willa had turned her head as if she could not stand having him step into her line of sight.

Matt sat on the bed next to her. She edged away from touching him.

"Willa, I know this is hard to believe right now, but it won't be like this all the time."

Her silence was deafening.

"You will heal and we'll give it another go. It will be better." God, he hoped it was. What a curse it would be to have a wife who could not tolerate his touch.

He would not let that happen. It was his responsibility to help her, to guide her. He was the one with the experience.

Leaning toward her, he said, "You liked what we were doing before." He had to remember that. She'd been extraordinarily responsive. This had led him to believe that her passion matched his own. He'd forgotten himself.

"It will be good between us." How many times had he already said this to her over the last two days? Now he prayed the words could be true.

Instead, she kept her back to him, hiding her face behind the blanket of her hair.

There was a knock on the door. He rose from the bed and answered it. Marshall himself stood with a cart. "There is brandy."

"Thank you," Matt said, taking the cart from him and rolling it into the room to leave the butler in the hall.

"I thought you might like to know the dowager has returned."

"Good," Matt said, his grandmother the last person on his mind.

"She was in good spirits. I take that to mean the wedding was a success?"

If only he knew. "Yes, it was. Breakfast on the morrow, served here."

"Yes, Your Grace. Have a good night."

Was it Matt's imagination or did Marshall almost give him a wink of brotherhood? He shut the door.

The repast he'd asked for was a cold one so that he and Willa wouldn't have to worry about when they ate. Of course, he'd made the request in an optimistic frame of mind.

He poured a healthy draught of the brandy in a glass and walked over to the bed. Willa huddled to the far edge. He knelt on the floor beside her, offering the drink.

"Willa," he whispered. She was probably thinking he was the worst pest. Well, he was. He had to help her through this. "Here is some brandy for you. I believe you should drink a bit."

Then they would talk.

He'd explain, apologize, promise—whatever he had to do.

What had happened between them had been inevitable, but they could not let this bad start be a mark against their marriage. Thinking about how she'd been so ready to give him the boot yesterday, he might need to do a good bit of convincing.

But he'd won her over once, and he would again.

"Willa?" He put a dash more imperative in his voice. "I need you to drink this. You will feel better."

Still, no response.

He dared to lift the curtain of her hair and was shocked to discover she had fallen asleep.

She slept like an exhausted child. Her hand was curled close to her lips and there were still tears on her cheeks. The sheets were damp with them.

"What a bloody bastard I am." Matt sat on the floor. Sleep was probably the best thing for her.

He glanced over at the cart of dishes and the bottle. The servants had placed a small vase of flowers upon it. They'd hoped to please their new duchess.

Matt lifted the brandy to his lips and drained the glass.

WAKEFULNESS CAME SLOWLY to Willa.

She felt heavy, as if drugged. She stretched her arms and tried to wake up. By the amount of light in the room, it was full morning. She arched. She could happily fall back to sleep, except she felt a very persistent call of nature.

Willa started to sit up, rubbing the sleep caked on her lashes, and that was when she realized that this was not her room—and she was completely naked.

Memory returned. His clothes were folded haphazardly on a chair. Her stockings were on the floor but she didn't see her dress. She had no idea where it had gone.

Worse, the air, her person smelled of *him*. The man whose big body took up most of the bed beside her.

He was sprawled on his back, a growth of whiskers darkening his jaw. His hair went every which way. A corner of the sheet covered him discreetly although his bare legs and chest were there for her view.

And she remembered everything.

Willa back-crawled out of the bed and came to her feet, wanting to put as much space between them as possible. There was something dry on her legs. She didn't want to think about what it was. She reached for the closest piece of clothing at hand, his shirt, and pulled it on. The hem went past her knees.

She was dragging the tangled mess of her hair out from the collar when Matt opened his eyes. He smiled sleepily, an endearing expression that she did not want to admire.

Any more than she wished to notice how shapely and masculine his long legs were.

Willa decided to give orders. "You must leave. I need a moment of privacy."

He rubbed his jaw and started to sit, pushing a pillow behind him. She prayed the corner of the sheet did not shift. She did not want to see his oyster bits.

"The chair is behind the screen," he said, and yawned.

"I require you to *leave*." She spoke softly, but firmly.

"I'm not leaving."

"Did you not hear me say I desire a moment of *privacy*?"

"You can have it," he replied, a touch irritably. "Behind the screen."

Willa truly needed relief . . . *however*—

"I can't do anything with you here."

"I'm not leaving," he answered, and crossed his arms as if to show he could be as stubborn as he thought she was.

She could have stamped her feet. "I want my *own* room." It was not an unreasonable request.

"Well, you can't have it. In my family, husbands and wives *share* the bedroom."

Willa narrowed her eyes at him. "Funny, I overheard your sister Kate inform you that in your family, husbands loved their wives, and you informed her that you didn't love me. Why are you standing on tradition now?"

If she'd slapped him, the response would have been little different. "You overheard that?"

Willa responded with a haughty shrug, not trusting the edge in his voice. "What does it matter?" she managed. "We aren't a love match." She almost choked on the words. She remembered everything from last night now—from the sheer bliss of his touch, to the knife-edged pain of his invasion of her body. What people had said was true. He had almost ripped her in half. She could never be a wife to him. She could not imagine what would happen if she carried his child. Why, there would be nothing left of her.

She forced herself to say clearly and distinctly, "We don't have to be together in this room. We are free to do whatever we want."

Matt's jaw tensed as if he wanted to speak and yet held back the words. Instead, he rose from the bed, heedless of his nakedness.

Willa tried not to look.

He picked up his breeches and put them on with quick, efficient movements. "Better?" The word dripped disdain.

"*Much*," she answered, surprised she could speak past the lump in her throat.

"But I'm not leaving this room," he said. "I won't," he answered her unspoken protest. "You will have to become accustomed to me."

"*Why?*" she ground out.

"Because we are married," he said. "You might already be carrying my child."

Willa thought she would be sick.

A knock sounded on the door. He moved past a tray of covered dishes that she was certain had not been there last night. "What are you doing?" she demanded.

"Answering the door. Or do you wish me to yell, 'Come in'?"

"You should put on more clothes."

He glared at her as if that had been the most priggish of statements. "I would, but you are wearing my shirt."

She was.

And she did not want anyone to see her in it. Furthermore, she could hold herself no longer. Her mind hurling every foul insult she could imagine at him, she dashed to the privacy screen, hoping that whoever was at the door would keep him from hearing her. With movement came an uncomfortable awareness of deep muscles she'd not known she'd had before.

And just the slightest hint of pain.

It was Annie at the door. "Good morning, Your Grace." To Willa listening behind the screen, the maid sounded nervous, as if the sight of the duke's bare chest was both disconcerting and highly improper. "I'm Annie, Her Grace's maid."

"I remember."

Her voice even more timid, Annie said, "I have your breakfast."

"Let me take the cart," Matt said, his grumbly voice sounding as if he was some dreaded beast from the innards of the earth. "You can roll the other one out. And order a bath. Make it the way my wife likes it."

A bath sounded like heaven. Willa was reluctantly glad he asked for one.

"Yes, Your Grace." There was the sound of movement and then Annie uttered a small cry.

Willa strained to hear what had happened.

"You can change the sheets on the bed as well," Matt said. "Take them away. Burn them."

"Yes, Your Grace," Annie replied, sounding chastened.

Willa believed she would die of the mortification. Especially when Annie dared, "Is Her Grace all right?"

"She is *fine*." Matt spoke as if "fine" was a sharp, pointy word.

There was the sound of sheets being wadded up. "Please call me if she needs me, Your Grace," Annie murmured, and then there was the rattle of dishes and a door closing.

Willa vowed she would never come out from behind this screen. She was going to stay here forever.

But she couldn't, especially as she caught the smells of fresh bread and even sausages. Her stomach rumbled. She'd barely eaten yesterday.

As she prayed that silence on the other side of the screen meant he'd left the room with Annie, hunger moved her out from behind the screen.

Her prayer had not been answered. Matt sat in a chair at the desk by the window. At the sight of her, he said, "My turn," like they were children playing a game.

He went behind the screen. Willa could hear him back there, just as he'd probably heard her. It was all too intimate, especially after last night. She sat in the chair he'd vacated, her back to the screen.

Matt came out with the chamber pot and walked to the door. He handed it to a maid who was out in the hall. He faced Willa. "There, that's done." He walked over and washed his hands in the basin. "Do you wish some soap?" he said.

She didn't move. "I don't like this."

"What, soap?"

"No."

"It's called marriage, Willa. We are married. Do you wish to wash your hands?"

Willa rose and walked over to the basin. She stopped and motioned him out of the way. He did not like that. For a second, there was a war of wills, but then he did step back. She scrubbed her hands well. "Thank you for ordering the bath."

He had already gone over to the cart and was lifting the covers on the food. "I thought you would like it. Hungry?"

Her stomach rumbled the answer.

He tried to hide a smile and she imagined how pleasant it would be to run over him with the cart. Instead, she admitted, "I'm starved."

"Cook is a far cry from your father's excellent chef, but she makes a good breakfast."

"I could eat raw meat right now," Willa said. She began filling a plate with sausage, fresh bread still warm from the oven, and a heap of butter. Taking silverware, she went over to the desk before returning for a cup of hot tea.

He had poured it for her.

Matt prepared a plate and joined her. For a good bit, there was only the sound of their eating. Food was a remarkable restorative.

When she was done, Willa set her silver down, and pulled her hair back. It would take an hour to untangle the ends. Matt was still shirtless. "Annie sounded a bit alarmed."

"By the sheets, yes. They weren't that bad. She is just concerned for you."

There was a knock on the door. Annie said, "Your Grace, I have the bath."

Willa jumped up from the chair and raced to the privacy screen as if hiding could divorce her from the humiliation of what had happened to her. She heard him swear under his breath and then called, "Come in, Annie."

Of course, Annie didn't carry up the bath alone. She had other servants with her. Willa listened to the noise of their pouring water into a tub. Her skin itched to be washed clean.

"Shall I stay and help Her Grace at her bath, Your Grace?" Annie asked.

"Your services will not be needed. I will let the hall maid know when we wish to have this all cleaned up."

"Shall I take the breakfast cart?"

"No, leave it there," Matt said. "My wife has a healthy appetite."

"She does," Annie readily agreed, a proud smile in her voice. "For such a wee thing, she enjoys her food." Almost as an afterthought, Annie tacked on, "Your Grace."

Matt laughed, the sound a far cry from his coldness moments ago. "Thank you, Annie." The door closed. He said, "You may come out of hiding."

Willa stepped into the room. The tub of steaming water looked marvelous.

"Annie made the bed," he said.

Only then did Willa glance at the four-poster. All evidence of what had happened to her was gone. She hadn't realized she'd been holding her breath until she released it.

"Will you now give me some privacy to enjoy my bath?" she asked.

He was sitting at the desk again, his large body relaxed, his long legs stretched forward in front of him so that she'd have to step over him to reach the tub. "No," he answered. "I won't."

Her temper flashed. "Matt, why are you doing this? Can't you tell that I don't want us to be this close?"

"We are man and wife. Willa. We *are* this close."

Her laugh was bitter.

He leaned forward. "I botched it last night. I hurt you. But be fair, Willa, before that horrible moment, I did please you."

Yes, he had. Which added to her sense of betrayal. "I didn't like it. You didn't stop."

"I couldn't, Willa. I'd reached a point I—"

His voice broke off. He seemed genuinely distressed.

Some of the hardness she felt toward him eased.

"I don't blame you for being angry," he said, his voice quiet, humble. "But the first time is always the worst. It will become better."

Willa didn't know if she believed him. However, the water in the tub was cooling. There was scented soap and several good linen towels. She longed for nothing more than to feel fresh. "You aren't going to leave me alone about this, are you?"

Matt shook his head. "I can't."

"Just because we are 'married'?" She shook her head. "You wanted my dowry, Matt. You have it. There is no reason to pretend that we are something more."

"I'm not pretending."

She almost scoffed at the idea.

He stood as if he'd heard her anyway. "Willa, I like you. I'm drawn to you. Will we fall in love? I don't know. But I do not believe you are indifferent to me, either. I'm not going to let what happened last night ruin what might be between us."

"Are you actually saying you *might* someday love me? If so, please don't put yourself out."

His brows drew together, and then he looked upward in frustration. "Why, God, have you surrounded me with headstrong women?" He turned back to her. "Are you going to use that bath? Or shall I?"

"I'm using it," she hurried to say.

"Then be on with it," he answered and began unbuttoning his breeches.

Willa took a cautious step back. "What are you going to do?"

"Serve as your lady's maid. I promised Annie. And I don't want to splash water on these."

Chapter 9

Willa was furious. Her eyes had taken on an unholy light of outrage.

But Matt wasn't going to back down.

He hadn't lied to her. In a short span of time, she'd taken over his imagination. His senses were aware of her in a way no woman had captured them before. He also knew if he bent to her wishes, she'd never come near him. She'd be like her mother, always lurking or attempting to escape the notice of her husband. That was not a marriage he wanted.

Taking off his breeches, he willed that arrant part of his body with its own mind to behave. No good would come from scaring Willa off.

The problem was that his reason and his lust were in conflict. His rodney, as his sisters affectionately referred to it, was like a divining rod searching for Willa.

"Matt, I don't need your help." She put the tub between them and crossed her arms. Did she realize how adorable she looked in his shirt that reached almost past her knees?

"You have it, whether you need it or not. Now, don't pay attention to him." He indicated his erection. "He is not trainable but I can keep him in line."

A strange look crossed her face. "Him?"

Matt shrugged. "It would be silly to call it a her."

She eyed it. "He isn't very attractive."

"No, he's not. However, he can do tricks."

"That's silly."

"I will have to show them to you someday. But right now, you bathe. Or I'm using the tub."

That hustled her. "I don't want you here." Her protest was a touch weaker.

"Willa, we've had this discussion. This room. You and me. We both belong here."

She could have run out the door. It was right there. But he was taking a gamble. Willa was not a coward.

And he'd wager that she wanted something *more* than cold disdain between them as well.

Waiting for her to warm up to him, and, yes, forgive him for last night, would be hard, but he was determined.

Willa glanced at the door, but she didn't move in that direction. Instead, she gave him her back. Her hands gathered the shirt hem and she took it off, revealing one of the loveliest backsides Matt had ever laid his eyes on.

Rodney agreed.

This was going to be a trial.

Crossing her arms so that she could cover her breasts and femininity, Willa hunched over protectively and stepped into the tub. She slowly sat down. She had to give up guarding her preciousness to move her hair out of the way. However, the tub was made for someone his size. The water was deep on her. She leaned forward, guarding herself, until a side glance enlightened her on the difficulty he was having with his little friend. She'd been so concerned, she hadn't noticed.

Now a sly look crossed her face.

"Willa, what are you thinking?"

"That this may be harder for you than it is for me." She lifted her arm away from her breasts. Rodney went full-out rigid. "Harder" had been the right word. He would never relax at this pace, and she smiled at Matt's struggle for control.

But she hadn't run.

Matt knelt beside the tub, feeling hoisted by his own rash claims. However, he was determined to be gentle and present. He wanted Willa's trust.

He picked up a cloth and dunked it in the water.

Willa caught his hand. "I can bathe myself."

With his other hand, he offered her the soap. She released her hold and took the scented cake, indicating with her gaze that he could remove his hand from her bathwater. He did, but he didn't move away from the tub.

She began lathering the soap on the cloth. "You don't need to stay right here."

"That is all right," he said, pretending he wasn't watching her every movement. "I like the floor."

Her nose twitched her suspicions. "It is awkward having you here," she murmured, washing her arms.

"That is a perception. Thousands of men and their wives share a room. It is all part of the intimacy of marriage."

Her lip curled. "What are you trying to do, Matt?"

"Be a good husband."

For a long moment she considered him and then she gathered her hair draped over the edge of the tub as if it annoyed her. "Please see if there is ribbon for my hair in a box on the wash-stand."

He was happy to do so, especially since Rodney had calmed down a bit. But he had to be careful. The little man was always ready to rise.

She pleased Matt when she said, "Would you help me tie my hair up?"

"A pleasure." He lifted the weight of it and wrapped it in a knot the way he used to watch his mother tie hers back. The ribbon would not hold it for long. "You have a good head of hair."

"I have too much hair."

"Cut it." He resumed his watch by the tub. He liked the view. The soap she was using smelled of lavender.

She moved as if less self-conscious around him.

Wiping the back of her neck with the cloth, she said, "I'm afraid to do so. I mean, some women, like your sisters, have shortened their hair, but—" She shrugged. "My father would never allow it." She drew the cloth down and looked to him. "Would you?"

Matt laughed. "I know better than to answer that question. A wise man doesn't tell a woman how to dress. Cut your hair, braid it, do what pleases you."

"But do you like it long?" She paused a beat and then said, "Last night, you seemed to enjoy taking it down."

Matt dared to lean an arm on her tub. She did not chase him away. "I'm more interested in you, Willa, not your hair."

She tilted her head in that manner she had whenever he seemed to say something that challenged what she believed.

He waited, hoping she would give him a little more insight into her thinking. Instead, she ran the cloth over her legs.

Matt would dearly love to take the cloth away from her. To have his hand be the one that spread lathered soap over her knees and around her calves.

Rodney stirred. And Willa noticed. She eyed him again with disfavor. "Does it always do that?"

"Apparently around you." And then, to take her attention off his discomfort, he reached in the tub and splashed water.

She gave a little yip as if his action was unexpected, and yet not unappreciated.

Slowly, with *great* patience, she seemed to be forgiving him.

Here was the price he had to pay for his loss of control. He had to make himself wait, even though he had a strong desire to lift her out of the tub, dripping wet, and make love to her right there on the floor.

But he held back . . . because she was worth it.

The realization that he might have married above himself—and he was not referring to her money—had started to come upon him watching her yesterday among the wedding guests. She'd moved with grace. He'd watched her listening to conversations, taking in Kate's boldness or someone else's gossipy or crass behavior. She'd kept her thoughts to herself, but she had been thinking. She was no one's fool. Including his.

"I'm finished with my bath," she said.

"All right." He picked up a towel, prepared to dry her off.

Her response was to snatch it out of his hand and wave him away.

He good-naturedly backed off. "Perhaps next time," he murmured.

"Perhaps."

Dear God, there was hope.

And he could ruin everything if he did as he wished and stared at her as she dried the water from her skin. Instead, he climbed into the tub.

The water was cool. Good. Cold as ice would have been better.

Willa went to the wardrobe and found a dressing gown on a hook. She put it on, sending a smile in his direction as if she had outwitted him. She began brushing her hair.

He didn't mind that she'd put on clothes. It was enough to know that she was naked under that scrap of material.

Naked and beautifully formed. He was a lucky man. He was also hard as a rock.

Matt picked up the bucket the servants had brought with the bath, filled it, and poured it over his head. His thoughts were not pure ones.

Especially once he caught her covertly eyeballing him. It made him want to give her a true show . . . that, and he didn't wish to climb out of the tub with what seemed to be, around her, a never-ending erection.

He also realized he didn't wish to smell like a lavender field. "There is a bar of soap by the washbasin. Would you hand it to me? It is in the shaving kit."

A simple request. She moved to do his bidding, picking up the soap and smelling it. "What is this fragrance? I always associate it with you. Sandalwood and what else?"

He held out his hand. "I don't know. It is something Alice and her husband blend for me. One of the many luxuries of knowing a chemist. It is their annual present to me. They have a scent for everyone in the family. They'll create one for you as well."

She placed the soap in his hand but didn't withdraw to the chair by the desk. Instead, she gracefully sat on the floor as he had and continued brushing the snarls out of her hair. "I wonder what it will be?"

"Something that will please you." Matt didn't dare draw notice to what he counted as a victory. This was a fragile truce between them. But also, he'd hurt her last night. She needed to heal.

He focused on scrubbing his body, splashing water everywhere. He didn't fit in the tub as neatly as she did.

Wiping water from his eyes, Matt squinted to see her holding a towel. "Thank you." He started to take it, but then paused. "Unless you wish to dry me off?"

Willa's answer was to jump up and go to the wardrobe. She made a great production of choosing what she was going to wear for the day . . . however, as Matt dried himself off, he knew she was aware of his movements.

Just as he was aware of hers.

He was disappointed, though, when she chose a dress and petticoats and disappeared behind the privacy screen. He took advantage of the moment to put on a pair of leather breeches, socks, and boots before starting to shave.

Willa came out from behind the screen. "You don't have a valet to do that?" The dress she'd chosen had a pattern of small flowers in shades of green.

"I will," he answered, rinsing his razor in the bowl before applying it again. Meeting her gaze in the looking glass, he said, "But I haven't had one. Fortunately, I could serve as my own. However, we will need to hire almost a whole new staff. I pray you are up for the challenge."

Her eyes widened in wonder as if she had not expected him to foist responsibility on her. He was pleased when she didn't back away from the idea but asked questions. As he shaved, he explained a bit about the state of Mayfield's outlying properties. She'd soon learn the full truth. He wiped the last of the soap from his face with a damp towel and motioned for her to turn around.

"What?" she said, balking . . . of course.

"Your laces are too loose." The dress was hanging from her.

"It is hard to reach back there. I was going to summon Annie."

"Let me help. Now turn." He made a circle in the air with his index finger.

She offered him her back, drawing her hair out of the way. As he pulled on her lacings, a memory came to him.

"When I was very little, sometimes I'd sneak to my parents' bed."

"Why?"

"Oh, because of a thunderstorm or a bad dream. Didn't you ever do that?"

"I couldn't. Their rooms were on a different floor than the nursery. They would not have appreciated it. If I'd done that, Annie would have been in trouble."

"She has been with you that long?"

Willa nodded.

He made a bow knot. "Well, our house didn't have floors. It was a thatched cottage and very cozy. But I remember watching my father do this for my mother. She'd move her hair just as you are, and he'd perform this small service." He lightly touched her shoulder to let her know he was done. "Thank you. It was a good moment to remember."

For a second, she stared at him as if he was some unknown entity.

And perhaps he was to her.

He'd been raised in a loud, loving family until death and school had pulled them apart. Still, his sisters had done all they could to keep contact with him, even challenging his grandparents' order that they were not to have access to him. They'd found a way.

Willa had no one. She'd never experienced living closely with another.

Matt moved to the wardrobe to find a shirt. Annie had unpacked Willa's things and he wasn't quite certain where she'd relocated his own clothes.

As he searched, he carefully said, "I know you will wish to make changes in the household. Especially this room. It should reflect your tastes."

"Do you believe your grandmother will let me?"

"She'll protest every change," he assured her with a smile. "But stand your ground, Willa. This is your home. I will support your decisions. The servants are already aware of who the mistress is."

WILLA WOULD BE lying if she said this morning had been easy. She'd wanted nothing more than to never see Matt again. Thoughts of the disaster of last night were enough to make her hide in shame. And anger.

She'd been led to believe it would all be fine. That she'd be as blissfully happy as Cassandra or Leonie, but that wasn't how it had been.

However, Matt was doing all he could to bridge the gap between them.

His way was softer than her father's would have been. Her father would have lashed out an order and expected to be obeyed.

Matt was allowing her a bit of breathing room. The walking around naked had been disconcerting . . . and yet, she'd grown a bit accustomed to it. Especially when he'd served as her lady's maid.

He'd not taken advantage of her, even when his base desire was so obvious.

And now, he was giving her the run of his household?

She had no doubt the dowager would bristle at some of the things Willa had seen needed to be done just in the hours she'd been in this house. She also remembered her disappointment in Mayfield. Both properties were antiquated. An interest in making changes rose inside her. Domestic matters had always appealed to her.

Matt was almost dressed. She searched for shoes. "What are we going to do today? Will we see your sisters?"

"They told me they were leaving," he answered with a shake of his head. "Kate rarely stays away long from her troupe. And Alice doesn't like to be apart from Roland more than a few nights."

"So it is just us?"

He nodded. "I thought it might be fun to see the sights of London. I've been too preoccupied since I gained the title to visit anywhere. You know the city far better than I. Where would you be going today if you could choose anywhere you wished to go?"

What an enticing idea. "Anywhere?"

"Besides shopping." He shuddered in distaste.

Willa knew exactly where she wanted to go. "Weeks Mechanical Museum. Have you heard of it?"

His eyes lit with interest and surprise. "I have, but I haven't been there."

"Neither have I, but I so wished to go. Father wouldn't let me. He said such things were not suitable for a lady. I've heard there is a huge spider there that moves as if it is alive. They call it a tarantula."

"I don't know if Weeks is the sort of a place for a lady," Matt said doubtfully, stating exactly what her father would have declared, before he added, "But it might be a perfect place for a duchess."

Willa wanted to throw her arms around him in delight—and she almost did but stopped herself in time. It would have been too familiar. Too bold.

But, oh, she wished she could let him know how happy he had just made her.

She practically danced as she finished her toilette. She hurriedly poked pins in her braided and heavy hair and expected her bonnet to keep it all in place. She grabbed her gloves and a shawl. It was going to be another lovely autumn day and she was anxious for the adventure.

Matt opened the bedroom door, allowing her to pass through first. Annie waited in the hall, and her anxious expression gave way to a smile when Willa made an appearance. "You look very fine this morning, Your Grace," she said to Willa.

"We are going to Weeks, Annie." Willa didn't know if Annie knew about the museum. Still, she had to tell someone. She liked saying it aloud. Finally, she could indulge her curiosity. Perhaps being married wasn't such a terrible thing.

"I pray you have a good day, Your Grace."

"We will, Annie," Matt said. "If we are back late, don't wait up."

"Yes, Your Grace." There was a happy note in the maid's voice.

Weeks was *everything* Willa had imagined. The mechanical tarantula that had been described to her numerous times was as frightening and fascinating as everyone claimed. And to believe there were real creatures like it—?

She soon learned that her husband's scholarly pursuits had included a smattering of all topics. He liked history, literature, and the sciences. The mechanics of the different creations interested him. He and other gentlemen visiting the museum began speculating about the workings of the wheels and levers. They tried to poke their noses around corners to see exactly what was going on.

The spider aside, Willa's favorite exhibit was a lovely swan swimming on a lake of glass and silver. The look in the bird's glass eye was lifelike.

As music played, the elegant swan moved its head left and right. Occasionally, it would stop and pause as if spying a fish in the water. Then it would actually bend its neck as if pretending to catch and swallow its dinner.

Afterward, because the day was still lovely, Matt and Willa walked down the street, enjoying the afternoon sun.

"Weeks was a grand adventure," Willa enthused. "Although I don't understand how they designed that one automaton"—one of the new words she had learned that afternoon—"of a lady blowing a horn."

"That was interesting," Matt agreed, however before he could say more, something ahead of them caught his eye. A crowd of children were gathered under the eaves of a house. A small girl was crying and the others were arguing loudly among themselves.

Matt moved ahead, Willa following.

"What is the matter?" he asked the crying child. She pointed up to the gutter where a black kitten with white feet clung precariously for its dear life. His frantic mews were heart-rending. He tried to pull himself up but lacked the strength.

A boy next to the girl said, "I told her we must let him fall. Cats have nine lives. Boots won't be hurt."

Willa could beg to differ. The drop was over two floors. She didn't see how such a wee kitten could survive.

"How did Boots end up there?" Willa asked.

"He climbed the tree," one of the other children said. "He's too afraid to go back." The tree was a horse chestnut whose limbs were close to the house. The kitten had apparently jumped to the gutter. For what purpose, no one knew.

Before she could offer an opinion, Matt handed her his hat. "I've done this before." He leaped for the tree's lowest branch, which was higher than anyone else could reach. Like an acrobat, he heaved himself up, carefully staying close to the trunk.

"Watch it," Willa warned. The limbs might not be able to support Matt's full weight. She didn't want to think what could happen.

His answer was a grin.

He moved up, testing the limbs as he did.

A woman who was actually a few inches shorter than Willa had come to her side. "Does he realize he is endangering his life for cat?" She held a hand up to shade her eyes against the sun so she could watch Matt climb.

"I believe he does," Willa said.

"Well, he is a better soul than I am. You children had best pray nothing happens to that gentleman."

"Yes, Mother," one of them said. The others were too intent on Matt's daring kitten rescue to answer.

He climbed out on a limb. The branches shook with his movements. Willa wasn't the only one holding her breath. He reached out. The kitten's hold on the gutter pipe had grown more tenuous until it seemed as if the poor creature was barely hanging on by a claw.

Matt stretched his arm. Boots cried loudly as if afraid of rescue, and then Matt's hand went around his scrawny middle. Paws flailed in the air as the kitten felt itself freed from the pipe.

A glad cheer went up. Willa was startled to see that beyond the children, they had gathered a crowd of onlookers. One man was even taking wagers on whether Matt would make it to the ground with the kitten successfully.

Anyone betting against her husband would have lost, she could have told him.

Matt swung down from the lowest branch, landing heavily. The kitten was not in his hand. The little girl looked expectantly at him and then burst into the happiest smile in the world when he reached inside his jacket and offered her Boots.

The children were well mannered. They shouted out thank-yous, looking at Matt as if he was a hero.

And he had been heroic.

How many gentlemen of his stature would have put themselves out for a kitten? Or noticed a crying child? London was full of them, and yet, he'd heard that extra note of distress.

The woman standing next to Willa said, "Thank you, kind sir. I could not have rescued our Boots. As you can see, I'm shorter than your lady. I'd gone upstairs to see if I could reach him from a window. No luck. I was about to give up."

"These are your children?" Matt said. Willa gave him back his hat, which he set at a rakish angle on his head.

"Most of them. Two sets of twins and two others. They are a handful. It is a pity my husband wasn't home. He's actually a bigger man than you. He could have saved our Boots."

"Well, I hope Boots has a long and happy life," Matt answered.

"And that he keeps his paws on the ground," the woman agreed. "Thank you again, kind sir."

Matt took Willa's elbow and, together, they walked away.

"You seem thoughtful," he said. "What are you thinking?"

Willa wasn't about to confess that she was a bit thrown off by the woman and her children. If her husband was close to Matt in size, well, those who had speculated on whether Willa could bear his child were wrong. All the children had appeared healthy and well-bred and their mother had been trying to save the kitten herself, which was exactly what Willa would have done . . .

She found his hand. His gloved fingers laced with hers.

"You aren't going to share what is on your mind?" he prodded.

Willa smiled up at him. He was truly handsome, but she was beginning to notice every slightest detail about him. He *wasn't* perfect, and that was good. He was as human as she, and he could admit to mistakes.

I botched it last night. I hurt you.

She still experienced some discomfort. Her muscles complained from time to time, but it was no longer a very big thing.

And, while Matt had laugh lines from the corners of his eyes, there were also shadows of worry and concern.

"I was thinking about how you like to rescue things," she said.

His brow came up. "Like the kitten?"

Like me. She smiled. "Among others."

For a moment, he acted struck by her words. "I suppose there is a protector in every male," he conceded slowly.

"Not every one," she could tell him. "My father is more of a competitor. He thrives on besting others."

"That, too, is a male trait."

Unbidden, Letty Bainhurst came to her mind. What had he said about her? That he'd believed he'd been rescuing her from a bad marriage?

He'd wanted to rescue Willa as well.

In fact, today, he'd been doing all in his power to help her feel safe.

Willa wondered if he saw a difference between her and Letty.

That she'd even had the thought made her angry—with herself.

Jealousy was an ugly emotion, and he'd given her no cause . . . and yet, where he was concerned, she was losing perspective. She was falling in love. And it had been effortless.

Had it happened as he sat beside her tub, obviously hungry for her and yet denying himself? Or was it because he'd been pleased to make her happy with a trip to Weeks?

Or had it been when he'd jumped to the ground from a horse chestnut tree with a kitten safely tucked in his jacket?

Actually, she'd started to fall in love with him when she'd read his book of poems.

The conversation she'd overheard yesterday between Matt and Kate came back to her. *I've been in love. It made a bloody fool of me. No, worse, it almost destroyed me. This is better. I respect Willa.*

That was what Matt had said.

Except walking down the street, her hand in his, Willa wanted the right to expect something more than respect. She wanted his love. She was far worthier of it than Letty Bainhurst had been.

They returned home. The sun was setting as they walked in the front door.

The dowager was in a flap. She'd obviously been waiting for them. "You aren't dressed," she said to Matt.

They had met her in the main hall. He'd just handed Marshall his hat. He spread his arms. "I obviously am."

"But not for Dame Hester's musicale tonight," Minerva retorted.

"I did not promise to escort you this evening," Matt answered. "And Willa and I have had long day."

"Matthew, you will be sitting in a chair all evening. The only thing you have to use are your ears."

"I will not go, Grandmother. Send for George. He likes those sorts of evenings."

"He is coming to ride with us," Minerva said.

"Then the problem is solved."

The dowager was not happy. Minerva shot a dark look at Willa, as if Matt's response was Willa's fault.

Upstairs in the bedroom, he apologized, "She is a bit of a bully. She wants to go everywhere, even though I am newly married and wish time with my wife."

"Perhaps you should go—?"

"No. Willa, she has to learn her place. We had a huge fight over her country party she hosts every year because she insisted on spending money I just did not have. She hammers me about realities she chooses to ignore. However, you and I have had a good day together. Is it wrong of me to want you to myself for a while longer?"

"I don't think so." Willa practically glowed from the idea he had enjoyed her company. "In fact, I'm claiming two points for keeping my husband to myself for another evening."

"Three points at least," he complained, and she laughed, earning herself a light kiss from him on top of her head.

They did share supper with Minerva, George, and another couple who were friends of the dowager's and of her age. George was good-natured about acting as Minerva's escort. Matt explained that George's own wife was not comfortable out in Society, and yet, it was important to his legal practice that he be seen.

The conversation at the table covered many topics from recent funding for the wars Britain fought on two fronts to whether or not all the fuss over Madam de Staël was sensible. Willa did not say much. Her father had refused to let her be anywhere close to Madam de Staël. She knew some of the issues before Parliament but had been taught the habit of not speaking her mind.

Every once in a while, Matt drew her into the conversation. Those moments were nerve-racking but only because few people, other than Cassandra or Leonie, had ever listened to Willa or asked her opinion. She'd been expected to be pleasant, poised, and polite. Her friends had been the bold ones.

But tonight, she felt something inside her begin to shift.

No one at the table mocked her observations. They had listened, and some had agreed.

She'd even disagreed with something Matt said. In fact, he changed his argument in favor of her thoughts.

There were few men who could do that, and she was married to one of them. The revelation was stunning. And those feeling of love grew stronger.

The company left. Before they went out the door, Minerva said, "Now, Your Grace"—Willa was starting to notice that Matt was *His Grace* to his grandmother when she wished to bully him and *Matthew* when she wheedled—"do not forget that I promised Diana Evanston you would be at her rout Saturday evening. With your duchess," she added, a tad sourly.

Matt looked to Willa. Of course, she knew of the Evanston ball. After her wedding breakfast, it was *the* invitation to be had. She nodded, and he said to his grandmother, "I have not forgotten. My duchess and I will be there." Willa had to stifle a smile. He liked referring to her as "my duchess" to his grandmother in particular.

And Willa found she liked him calling her his "my" anything. She moved closer to him.

Minerva and her friends went out the door. They were all taking the Camberly coach. However, George hung back.

Seeing that there was a moment of privacy, he leaned close to Matt and said, "I have done what you asked about that matter we discussed. Men have been hired."

Matt's manner grew serious. "Good. Thank you."

"Are you certain you don't wish to let this go?"

"I'm certain."

"Be careful." On those words, George left.

"Men have been hired for what?" Willa asked.

"Work around the estate," he answered with an air of distraction.

Instinctively, Willa questioned what he said, and then chided herself. True, why would a lawyer be involved in hiring workers? However, was she going to become one of those women who hovered over her husband's every word? She prayed not.

"Sherry?" Matt asked.

"Are you having anything?"

"Port."

"Then I will enjoy a glass of sherry with you."

The day had been long. The preceding night had been even longer, except now it was just a memory. Willa could almost pretend last night hadn't happened.

She and Matt sipped their drinks by a fire in the private sitting room. She kept yawning and he took pity on her and led her to their bedroom, where, to her surprise, he turned her over to Annie.

The maid brushed out her heavy hair and made quick work of braiding. She carried over a nightdress for Willa.

Like all of Willa's nightgowns, this one was of heavy material. Annie dropped it over Willa's head and arms.

There was a knock at the door and then Matt let himself in. Annie went scurrying away.

And they were alone again—in *this* room, which Willa realized was becoming a bit of a sacred place to her.

He began undressing. Annie had turned down the fresh sheets, and Willa walked over to sit on the bed, very aware of every piece of clothing he removed.

Matt didn't wear nightclothes.

"When you have a valet, we will have to work out a routine," she said. Her voice sounded a bit breathless.

"We will." He walked over to other side of the bed from her. "Tired?"

"A bit." There was a pause. The mattress stretched between them. "I'm glad we didn't attend the musicale."

"We will *never* attend one of Dame Hester's musicales." He climbed into the bed, pulling the sheet over his hips. "Joining me?"

It wasn't the bed that was holding her back.

It was the barrier she wore. The gown weighed heavy on her. And this was not how she wanted to be with her husband. Willa took off the gown.

She was rewarded by his smile and a quiet, "Come here."

It was funny that she'd never known her heart could make a little leap in her chest before. He was going to wish to be intimate again. She would not like the pain, but as her mother said, this was the sacrifice women made. She might try counting backward. She climbed in the bed, and Matt drew her closer to him.

He kissed her. Their lips melded together as if it was the most natural thing in the world. He rolled her on top of him, her breasts against his hard planes, her hips on his, her braid over her shoulder. He was ready for her.

The kiss deepened.

Willa was starting to learn the signs of her body. She was preparing for him, and yet, she was anxious. If letting him hurt her was what must be done—

To her surprise, Matt moved her over to his side, her back against him, his hips curving around her buttocks. "Go to sleep, Willa," he whispered in her ear.

"But you—"

He shushed her. "Yes, I want you." He ran his hand over the curve of her hip and down her thigh. "You are lovely, Willa. But it is too soon for you. It will happen between us. I'm willing to wait until it is as pleasurable for you as it will be for me."

Willa didn't know if that time would ever arrive.

And yet, it was very nice to be held this way. To feel protected and valued.

When she fell asleep, she dreamed about children.

MATT LAY AWAKE watching Willa sleep, a sign that she trusted him.

He moved her braid so that it wouldn't catch under his body and wake her.

He felt humbled. Today had been fun. His petite wife had a lively intelligence.

Yesterday, at the wedding celebration, Soren had taken him aside to tell him that he was a lucky man. That Willa Reverly would be the sort of wife who would be an honest companion. She would enhance his life, he'd said. "And bring out the best in you."

"You are telling me this because . . ." Matt had prodded, a touch offended.

Soren had given him a hard look, an exasperated one. "Because I fear you don't realize how bloody fortunate you are. You believe your title is a gift to her, and in exchange for the money her father has settled upon you. But the truth is, Matt, Willa is a far better woman than you deserve."

At the time, with the headiness of the wedding celebration around him, Matt had shrugged off his groomsman's comments. Although it wasn't like Soren to give advice.

Now, beside Willa in bed—and remembering her gratitude toward him after she'd finally seen the tarantula or the admiration in her eyes when he handed the kitten over to the child—Matt realized Soren might be right.

The expression on Willa's face had made him feel heroic.

I was thinking about how you like to rescue things. That was what she had said. Her comment had summed him up.

Ever since his earliest memory, he'd wanted to make the world right. To please everyone. His parents' back-to-back deaths had only reinforced his need to take care of those close to him. And when the circumstances were impossible, well, he wasn't his best self.

However, watching the sleeping woman beside him, he realized he had lost his way some time ago. Well before Letty.

As a boy, he'd been caught between loyalty to his sisters and absent grandparents whom he'd felt obligated to please, but never could.

At last, he understood what Soren had been saying.

His behavior before the wedding toward this vibrant woman had been boorish. She was giving him a second chance . . . and she might be the person to help him become the man *he* wished to be. She had the strength of character to both test and challenge him, and he found he always wanted her to look at him as she had that afternoon when he'd rescued the kitten.

Always.

Chapter 10

The next several days were idyllic for Matt. He was now doing what he should have been doing before the wedding—he was learning to know his wife.

They spent time with Dewsberry and his countess before they left for Cornwall. There were jaunts to museums and exhibits and a night at the theater. Everything was light and relaxed.

Willa asked if they could attend a performance of Kate's troupe, even if they had to travel a bit. Matt was ashamed to admit it had been years since he'd attended one of his sister's plays. Another failing of his brought to light. "After the Evanston rout, we'll search out where her troupe is."

They also spent two days at Mayfield. Matt proudly introduced Willa to his tenants. He was also pleased to share what he'd learned about agriculture and the details of his estate. See, he wanted to say about those months in the country, he hadn't just been pining for Letty Bainhurst, he'd been trying to do good.

He didn't know why he thought of Letty in that moment, except he sensed part of Willa's shyness around him was because of the infamous affair. She didn't bring it up, but there were times she nailed him with her direct insight and other moments when he sensed she held back.

They slept beside each other. Willa no longer questioned the practice and she seemed relaxed with his presence, a sign of trust, he hoped . . . because his regard for her grew with every passing day.

His self-inflicted celibacy had heightened his awareness of her. It also meant he had to truly pay attention to her. And there were moments, especially when she slipped her hand in his, that he felt a contentment he'd never experienced before. Since he first attracted the notice of women, they had let him know they liked the way he looked. He'd rarely had to work for their approval.

But he had to work for Willa's. And she demanded more than those women had. She valued character. She was remarkably perceptive to the smallest nuance, and yet guarded. He didn't understand the roots of her doubts. He knew it wasn't because of her rough initiation into sex. She didn't seem to hold a grudge against him; however, he was determined to use his better nature to please her.

The morning of the Evanston rout, the one Minerva had hounded them over, they went on a picnic by the River Lea and did a bit of fishing. Willa wasn't missish at all. She baited her own hook and even attempted to push him into the water. Their laughter had echoed around them.

Later, Matt fell asleep under a tree, his head in her lap. He woke to the sound of her humming. She looked down at him and gave a contented smile.

Matt had an urge to turn his head where it rested and sample what he wanted—except it was too soon for such a bold movement. He believed her passions matched his but he was waiting for her to make the first move.

"Did your cousin George send those men you wanted to hire for work?" she asked, interrupting the carnal direction of his thoughts.

She referred to his hushed conversation with George the other night. He had hoped she'd forgotten it. Instead, she seemed to remember everything.

"What did you want them to do?" she asked.

"It is of no importance," he answered.

"George behaved as if it was important."

Matt sat up. He looked at her . . . and realized he could share the truth. She was his wife. The results of Hardesty's blackmail affected her. It was the whole reason he'd married her.

What if she heard the story from someone else? What conclusion might she draw against him?

"It was a matter about money that everyone, including George, believes I should abandon."

Willa straightened up to truly hear what he was saying. "Do you think the matter should be abandoned?"

He looked at her sitting beneath the spreading oak, a bit of color to her cheeks and her hair in a braid over one shoulder, and answered, "Right now, in such a peaceful setting, it does seem silly to pursue it."

"Why? What was the issue?"

Matt shifted his weight. "My grandfather was being blackmailed."

"Blackmailed?" she repeated in disbelief. "Over what?"

"The reason isn't important." He wasn't going to talk about his uncle William. Let the dead have their peace. "It stopped almost two years ago but by then the estate was robbed dry."

"That's what happened?" She flipped her braid over her shoulder. "People speculated about why your family had lost their money. Father assumed it was poor investments. He didn't know what kind. He looked into it."

"Being cautious, I suppose."

"When it comes to money, Father is always wary. Money is his purpose in life. So, why did you want to hire the men?"

"The name of the blackmailer is Hardesty. I had some thought to track him down. I would like to have back what we lost. Or at least find justice."

"And now?"

He thought a moment. "For the honor of the title, I should hunt the man down. It is what is right. However, perhaps everyone is right. Perhaps, I should just count myself incredibly fortunate."

"Because you have my money."

There was a clip to her tone, a challenge. Cautiously, Matt said, "It has helped."

"And now justice doesn't matter."

Yes, there was definitely a troubling undertone. "I didn't mean that *you* don't matter, Willa."

She abruptly came to her feet. "That is all right." She dusted the dirt and grass from her skirts, not meeting his eye. She swept up her wide-brimmed hat and set it on her head. "We aren't a love match. Come, we should return. It will take me hours to prepare for my debut as a duchess this evening. Will I truly have to be presented at court?"

"Soon, yes." Minerva had her secretary making arrangements.

"It seems a great deal of fuss for nothing." She began walking toward the two-wheeled gig he had hired for the outing.

Matt came to his feet and bounded after her. His long legs ate up the ground between them. He fell into step beside her, shortening the length of his stride. "What is the matter, Willa?"

She didn't look at him but continued purposefully forward as she tossed out, "Nothing. It's all fine."

He sensed it wasn't.

Matt took her arm. "I've offended you."

A look crossed her face, one he couldn't decipher. She didn't answer.

"Willa, please, what did I say?"

She didn't want to have this conversation. She glanced at the gig only five feet away. The horse was asleep, one hoof cocked. Like any hired nag, it was not anxious to wake.

And that was when Matt gathered his courage and asked, "What if we had been a love match?"

That caught her attention. A calmness seemed to settle over her. She closed her eyes, her dark lashes fanning her cheeks. She took a deep breath and released it before opening her eyes and saying, "I wish we had been a love match."

"We could be," he heard himself say.

"If we *loved* each other," she answered carefully.

And here was the moment when he should declare himself to her. He could imagine his sisters watching and silently urging him to do what was right. Except he couldn't say he loved Willa.

He'd loved Letty, and his feelings had been a constant turmoil. His world had circled around her. When she'd left him, he'd been shattered.

Matt never wished to let himself be that vulnerable again.

"I hold you in the highest regard."

Disappointment crossed her face. "I understand." She turned and walked to the gig. She climbed in, taking her seat.

Matt followed. "Do you?"

She scrunched her nose as if confirming she did. "Yes. I believe you are saying that I won't ever measure up."

"Wait—no, Willa, I'm not saying that at all—"

Willa stopped his flow of words with her fingers across his lips. "You've been kind. I appreciate that you haven't forced yourself on me."

Forced. He did not like the way that word sounded. It offended him. "It shouldn't be 'force' between a man and his wife."

"You know what I meant, Matt."

Actually, he didn't. "We will make love again, Willa. I can't promise it won't hurt. I'm a big man."

And what if it did? His every intention was to honor his marriage vows. Could he go through life married to a woman as lovely and charming as Willa, and remain celibate? "Make love," she echoed. "Interesting choice of words. Especially since love can mean so many different things. I don't want anything from you that isn't freely given, Your Grace. That is, anything save your honesty. I always want honesty from you, Matt." She moved over on the seat. "We need to return home. We mustn't be late for the Evanston rout. Minerva would be greatly disappointed. She has made all the plans." She spoke as if what they'd been discussing did not matter, and yet, it did.

He stood there a moment more, scanning his mind for something he could say. He wanted to return to their earlier contentment.

"Willa, perhaps given time—"

She held a hand up. "No, don't give me banalities."

"But I admire you." He did. After the raging passion he'd been through with Letty, Willa was a cool, refreshing spring. She was clear-eyed and uncomplicated.

"I admire you as well, Your Grace." She could have been speaking to anyone, and it made him angry.

Matt untethered the horse, a sign to the mare that her nap was done. He climbed into the gig. It swayed in his direction as his heavier weight took a seat beside Willa. They were thigh to thigh.

But he didn't move the horse on.

Instead, he sat. And she sat waiting.

Then she broke the silence. *"My lover's kiss is like no other, an answer to my soul. On a bed of roses, we joined, finding our peace in each other.* Do you recognize the words?"

He feared he did. "I wrote them. Bad poetry."

"I don't agree. I thought it noble and proud. When I read what you'd written, I said to myself, here is someone who understands what love truly is."

"Actually, I wrote the book as a way to honor my parents. It is what I'd observed about them. Not the sexual parts. Those were merely the fevered yearnings of a young man who thought himself a poet."

"Or who believed in a love that was above all others." She turned to him. "You are fortunate. My parents have never moved me to poetry. Or to emulate them in any way." She turned away, looking straight ahead. "So, here we are. Two people who don't quite know what love is."

"I know it can eat you up inside. That it can be soul crushing."

"That wasn't what you wrote, Matt. Perhaps you would be wiser to trust the younger you. Now, can we go home? I need a bit of time."

"To prepare for tonight?"

"No, to lick my wounds."

For the first time since he'd confronted her the afternoon before their wedding, he sensed a barrier being built between them, and he didn't know what he should do.

So he drove her back into the city.

They were almost in sight of the house when Willa said, "I'm glad you told me of the blackmail. It explains much."

"Do you think I should leave it be?"

She looked at him. "I think each of us has to do what we individually think is right."

He didn't believe she was talking about Hardesty.

The strength of his parents' love for each other came to mind. It had been an unbreakable bond. One that he'd longed to have in his life. He knew it had called for great trust between his parents. Or had they just been lucky? There was the mystery.

He'd thought he'd found that strong a love once, and now, because of his own foolishness—no, weakness—he felt sad that he might not have it with Willa.

IF MATT HAD his way that evening, he would have stayed home. He and Willa. Their conversation had unsettled him. He didn't like the way he felt about himself.

However, he also needed to introduce his duchess to Society. Minerva was correct in announcing that it would be a good event for him and Willa to attend.

He gave the bedroom over to Willa and Annie. They, too, understood that this evening would be the Duchess of Camberly's debut in Society. The primping went on for a good two hours.

However, as Willa made her way down the steps to join him waiting with Minerva in the front hall, Matt could say their time had been well spent.

Willa was always lovely to him but, tonight, with her hair piled high on her head and wearing a dress of cream gauze trimmed in gold ribbons and lace, she was spectacular. She wore a delicate, long gold chain around her neck and kid gloves up to her elbows. Her every gesture was feminine grace.

Watching her, something deep within him began to open.

"See?" his grandmother said quietly behind him. "I would not suggest just anyone for you to marry. Not for the title."

How like one of his grandparents to take full credit for the marriage, and yet, it was true. She'd prodded him to ask for Willa and now he could confirm it was the wisest decision of his life.

He met Willa at the stairs, taking her gloved hand. "Every man will be jealous of me this evening."

She blushed, and he wanted to take her right back upstairs and have his way with her.

Most of all, he wanted to turn back time to before they'd been so honest with each other.

They set off for Evanston's home. There was a queue of coaches and vehicles waiting to release their passengers at the front door. Matt's driver and footman shouted to make way for the Duke of Camberly. Evanston's servants quickly waved them forward. The other guests whose places they had supplanted craned their necks as if trying to look into their coach. Matt knew they were anxious to claim the first glimpse of his duchess.

A servant opened the coach door at Evanston's front step. Matt jumped out and then helped the ladies.

Inside, the ballroom was a crush of people. It took a good ten minutes for Matt and his ladies to make it from the step to inside the front door and the receiving line.

Lady Evanston was considered a leading hostess. She was a willowy woman with a slender face and a braying laugh. She happily informed Matt's party that she had christened the evening "an Adventure in Greece."

To that end, giant Greek boats made of paper, wood, and glue had been hung from the ornate ceiling so they seemed to float in the air above everyone. More than one gentleman whispered that he prayed they didn't come close to any candles. Meanwhile, male servants in Evanston livery wore Minotaur masks that covered their whole heads and shoulders, as if they were hairy beasts.

The room hummed with the voices of men and women greeting one another while musicians readied themselves for dancing.

Minerva immediately noticed a group of her friends. She turned to Matt. "I'll see you at supper." She referred to the light meal that would be served around midnight to fortify guests at a ball such as this. Matt could only imagine how much food it would take to feed this army of guests.

"Well, now we are free to do whatever we wish." He let his hand find Willa's. "How many points for a dance?"

"Three."

"I wonder if I can earn at least fifteen points this evening?" he asked.

Willa shot him a sly look. "It might be possible. I understand the duchess is overly fond of you."

He laughed, and suddenly realized he could fall in love with her. It would be different from what he'd felt for Letty. Their liaison had been filled with drama and secretiveness. There had been anticipation and heady excitement. What he was feeling for Willa was vastly different.

Matt kissed the back of her hand, a gesture, he noted, that was caught and then catalogued by many around them for possible gossip on the morrow.

He proudly led Willa to the dance floor. Other couples were just taking their places for the opening set. They nodded their welcome to Matt and Willa, and he was able to introduce her to the few people he knew.

As he had expected, many gentlemen were envious of him.

However, Matt was *claiming* her. And it did feel good to not have to hide his connection with Willa, to not skulk around the way he had with Letty, lest her husband find out about them. It was freeing. Honorable. The way a relationship should be.

He focused on Willa and on dancing and enjoying the role of being in demand by all the glittering people around him. He and his new wife moved from one social group to another as introductions and reacquaintances were made. The tension between them since their conversation earlier in the day eased.

Several times, Willa helped him by quietly mentioning the

names of people around them that he had forgotten. This enabled him to please many that he remembered who they were. He appreciated her help.

They had just finished a Scottish reel, part of his intention to earn fifteen points, when Willa held up her hand. "I heard it was one point for a cup of punch."

"Is that all? I prefer the higher point activities."

She nudged him with her shoulder for his failure to take her hint. "Very well, two points for a cup of punch."

He placed his hand at the small of her back and looked around for a servant with a tray of drinks. He wasn't finding one. "I'm not ready to leave your side. I need to make up for all those evenings you attended these events alone."

"I don't feel lonely this evening. I feel like the Duchess of Camberly. And she is a very fortunate woman."

If a white light had come down from heaven and shone on him, Matt could not have received a better blessing.

A voice inside him asked how easy it would be to whisper *I love you* to this beautiful woman. A week ago, even that morning, he'd doubted love existed. But now? What if love wasn't a grand, passionate, overwhelming emotion but a quiet serenity and a sense of peace? Such as what existed between Soren and Cassandra? Or Alice and Roland?

Could love be something as simple as helping his wife with her lacings?

Lady Bettina had struck up a conversation with Willa. She was quickly joined by two other young women. It was obvious they were attempting to curry Willa's favor.

Unable to find a servant with a drink tray, Matt excused himself. "I will fetch a cup of punch," he promised. Willa nodded and he was off.

The punch table was very busy. He was halfway to his destination, skirting the dance floor, when one of the Minotaur-dressed footmen bumped into him.

"Sorry, Your Grace," the servant said, even as he slipped a small folded noted into Matt's gloved hand. The Minotaur didn't hesitate but kept on his way.

Curious, Matt moved toward the wall, away from prying eyes, and opened the letter—

I wish a meeting. I'll be waiting. The side hall, third door on the left.

Hardesty

The bastard was here?

Matt stared in shock at that signature written in an upright scrawl, and forgot about punch cups. Hardesty was contacting him—just as everything in Matt's life was working to his benefit.

Just as Matt had come into money.

Did Hardesty think to blackmail him? For a second, Matt was tempted to ignore the summons.

He knew he could not.

Using his height to his advantage, he could see Willa was still busy with Lady Bettina. There was time for a brief, and brutal, encounter with Hardesty. Then he would pick up her cup of punch and return to her.

Matt pocketed the note and went in search of the side hall.

He stopped a servant, one not wearing a Minotaur head. "Where is the side hall?"

The servant explained that two halls ran parallel to the ballroom. One was the main hallway where the guests had entered the house. The other was quieter. The card rooms had been set up there. His Grace could not miss it. What the family called the side hall was off that hallway.

Matt had no trouble finding the card room. It was well marked and very busy.

He noticed his cousin George was sitting at one of the tables. They waved at each other. Willa's mother was there as well, although he didn't try to catch her attention.

Matt almost took a moment to tell George about the note, but then his cousin tossed several coins onto the table, and he reconsidered. George was serious when he played. He would not appreciate the interruption.

Matt found the side hall.

The note said the third door.

It was closed.

Matt stood outside it a moment and then didn't bother to knock but barged right in, his fist doubled and his every nerve ready for anything.

The room was a small sitting room. A lamp burned on a table beside one of several chairs. It cast a warm glow around the dark green walls that gave the setting intimacy.

Standing on the far side, as if to keep the chairs between her and the door, was Letty Bainhurst. Golden, privileged, and exquisite in her beauty.

Matt was caught off guard.

She didn't appear to be surprised. She acted as if she'd been waiting for him. With a glad cry, she ran toward him.

Chapter 11

Stunned by the sight of Letty when he'd had no reason to expect her, Matt didn't react until the weight of her body hit his. Her arms banded around him, tightening their hold.

The heady scent of her perfume swirled around him, reminding him of her most intimate places. Her curves melded against him. How many times during their illicit meetings had she run at him in exactly this manner? His arms naturally wrapped around her—but in his defense, his common sense was shouting, *Damn.*

Letty kissed his neck and chin. Matt had the presence of mind to lean back, both to avoid her and to close the door behind him.

"You haven't forgotten me," Letty whispered fervently between her kisses. "You *haven't.*"

He attempted to release her hold of him. She wasn't cooperating. Her body, which had always understood his far better than he did, rubbed intimately against him while her lips went for his mouth.

He tried to tell her to leave off, but the words caught in his throat and came out in a groan of frustration . . . which sounded very much like pleasure.

Her breasts pressed against his shirt. Even through the layers of clothes, he could feel her hard nipples, smell the readiness of her . . . He remembered so much about her—

And then he thought of Willa.

Willa, who was spun gold to Letty's dross. If his wife caught
him here—

Matt pushed Letty away. He held her at arm's distance. Her lush
pink lips puckered and made silly fish noises as she begged for
his kiss.

Dear God. Had he once found this exciting?

Matt let go and stepped away, moving around the edge of the
room.

Letty gave her head a shake, her blond curls bouncing, as
if she had just realized he was not holding her. She whirled
to face him, her brows coming together in a frown. "You are
angry with me."

"Angry? No. Wary. You are the one who informed me *I* was
unnecessary."

Her stance softened. She raised a hand to her head as if confused and said, "I know, I know, I know." There was something
that appeared to be sincere regret in her large, green eyes as she
confessed, "I wronged you. I should never have let you go. It was
cowardly of me." She took a step toward him. "My husband came
very close to finding out about us, and I needed to separate myself
from you. I believed I was saving you from Bainhurst's wrath. I
know I didn't handle the matter well. I was unkind." She came
another step closer, her hands held out in the pose of supplicant.
"Letting you go was huge mistake. Matt, I think about you every
waking hour. I dream of you."

Even as little as a week ago, those would have been blessed
words to Matt's ears. He'd wanted a declaration from her. He'd
certainly made many to her.

In the close space of this room, he realized she had been nothing more than his Achilles' heel. He'd been floundering with the
responsibilities of the title and overwhelmed by a failing estate.
Letty had made him feel worth something—and Hardesty had
known Matt's weakness. Why else would he have sent a note
guiding Matt to her? Hardesty might have even orchestrated the
whole affair with Letty.

The thought caught Matt off guard, and yet, there was evidence of the possibility.

When he and Letty had parted company at his grandmother's country party, Letty had shown no remorse. She'd been cold-hearted and had behaved almost as if she couldn't wait to be away from Matt.

Furthermore, their romantic trysts had begun almost immediately after they met. Letty had been the seducer. She'd said things that had stirred what Willa had called Matt's need to be the rescuer.

What better accomplice could a blackmailer have chosen?

"Matt?" Letty was a step away from him.

He grabbed her by her arms, holding her at bay. "What do you know of Hardesty?" he demanded. He was glad his voice was steady. "Why are you here and not him?"

"Hardesty?" She frowned. "I don't know anyone named Hardesty."

"Perhaps your husband does?"

"He might. He knows many people. Matt, why are you asking me about this man? And why are you looking at me as if I am guilty of something?"

"Why are you *here*?" he responded.

That set her back.

She took a step back, yanking her arms away from him. She reached into the bodice of her gown and pulled out a note. "I'm here because *you* requested this meeting."

"Let me see that." Matt unfolded the note. It was written on the same kind of paper as the one he had received. The handwriting was nothing like his own, except that Letty would not have known. Matt had never written to her. Notes could have been found by her husband.

"This is not from me," he said. "When did you receive it?"

Letty rubbed her arms where he'd held her as if he'd hurt her. He hadn't. "Shortly before I left for dinner with friends this evening. Say, half past seven. Perhaps even eight. *You* didn't send it?" She didn't quite believe him.

"Letty, I didn't know you were in town."

Her frown deepened. "I was bored of the country and returned several days ago. Your wedding day, in fact." She made a face as if she'd known and was unapologetic that it was perhaps more than just happenstance. That maybe he should be flattered?

"And, since I was in town," she continued, "I knew I must attend my good friend Diana's ball." Diana was Lady Evanston. "I confess, I had heard rumors that you were happy with your little wife. I'd begun to fear you had forgotten me, until that note."

Was Hardesty watching all of them?

It did not seem possible. How could any stranger be that close to all of them—unless Hardesty was not the man's true name?

"Does your husband know about us?" Bainhurst was a power-ful lord. They said he brokered in secrets. And yet, for all the people who knew about Matt and Letty, Bainhurst had suppos-edly never known. That didn't make sense.

She shrugged. "I don't know. The man is maddening. He seems to enjoy being jealous. What is this about, Matt? If you didn't send that note, who is it from?"

It was on the tip of his tongue to answer what little he knew, and then he remembered Letty was not his friend. He could not count on her. It had been a hard lesson.

"I don't know," he answered. "That is the puzzle."

Her lower lip curled into a childish pout. "In truth, my only question is about us. I don't care who sent the note. I was happy to receive it. However, I sense you've had a change of heart even though you had promised to love me even when I couldn't believe in us."

Dear God, he could spout some drivel. "Letty, there can be nothing between us. I'm married." There, he'd said it—and he felt rather noble.

"Are you saying you wouldn't have married if I hadn't set you free?" Her pout turned into a sly smile as if he'd put forth a chal-lenge. "There was something between us just a moment ago." She took a step in his direction. "Besides, after everything is said and done, you did come here for me."

"No, I came to see a man named Hardesty—" He stopped, struck by a new idea. "Or he could be a woman. I have no description of the actual person."

"You are saying your Hardesty could be me?" She laughed.

He didn't.

Her laughter stopped. "You can't be serious?" She shook her head. "Matt, who is this Hardesty to you?"

"Someone I was hoping to meet." He still held her note in his hand. "I'm keeping this."

"Of course." She slid her hand into her bodice over her left breast and flipped the thin material over to reveal her breast, sliding her hand beneath it. "In fact, you can have whatever you want from me."

This was a dangerously compromising position. "Letty, I'm leaving."

She moved to place herself between Matt and the doorway. "You will have to go by me first." She smiled her confidence in her power over him, and it made him angry. She'd played with his heart, she'd caused him to doubt himself, and now she wanted him to believe that her feelings were true?

"Out of the way, Letty." He moved forward. He'd walk over her if necessary.

She wasn't going to let him go. She reached for him, grabbing his coat. "Matt, please. I don't know this Hardesty. But I want a second chance." She dug in her heels as if daring him to drag her. He turned, trying to escape. Her hand went for his neck as if to catch and hold him. "I was trying to protect you, Matt. Bainhurst can be vicious when he's crossed. Don't hold my love for you against me—"

The door opened. Light from the hall spilled into the room. Willa stood framed in the doorway.

The three of them froze. "I—I didn't knock, did I?" Willa said, and then answered her question, "No, I did not."

Without another word, she turned on her heel and left.

Matt swore and went after her. Letty tried to catch his arm, but he shook her off. He didn't bother being gentle.

Out in the hall, Willa moved at a furious pace, her skirts swaying. He didn't know why she tried to run. His one step could easily overtake her three. He caught up with her before she reached the adjoining hallway.

"It is not what you think," he said.

She stopped so abruptly, he took a step past her. "It doesn't matter what I think." Her voice was tight. "It is what I *saw*." She neatly stepped around him and would have charged off, but he hooked his hand in her arm.

"You must listen. Letty means nothing to me. *Nothing*."

But his words didn't mollify her. Her eyes alive with anger, she said in a furious whisper, "Don't play these games with me. I've spent a lifetime listening to my father lie to the people closest to him about his meetings with women who were not his wife—"

"Willa, you have it wrong. I was not having a tryst with Lady Bainhurst." He kept his voice low. He was aware there were those who could overhear. "Hardesty—" he started to explain, but she was not in the mood to listen.

"My father's current mistress is younger than I. I caught them out shopping several weeks ago. He told me that it wasn't what it seemed, because he dotes on his image but he has no substance. And I remembered all the times he'd tell my mother that she was making up her suspicions, that she was being possessive." She straightened her shoulders. In that moment, she could have been as tall as Matt. "I have seen what he has done to my mother and *I will not live that life*. I want *more*."

"I am prepared to give you more," Matt said, suddenly realizing what was truly behind Willa's desire to jilt him. Her caution. Her doubts about him. He'd made a cake of himself over Letty. In Willa's shoes, he would have been careful. "You can trust me."

She shook her head. "If I'd caught you with anyone but Letty Bainhurst, it might not hurt so much. But I'd started to believe you, Your Grace. I'd fallen in—"

Willa broke, not finishing the thought. "I have to leave." Her voice was charged with tears.

He grabbed her arm. "You've fallen into what?" he demanded. "What were you going to say?"

"It doesn't matter, Matt. None of this matters because I won't let myself fall in love with you. Ever." She slipped under his arm and out of his hold. She practically ran from him.

Matt felt gutted.

Willa had loved him? Even though he wasn't the perfect lover, she'd started to fall in love with him.

And he *loved* her. He didn't even know why he'd entertained doubts. No woman had captured his imagination the way Willa had. He was a better man with her than he'd ever been at any time in his life.

"*What* a ninny," Letty's voice drawled behind him. "I can't believe she would carry on because we were together. You might be better off without her."

"I'll be damned before I touch you again." Matt began walking after Willa. He would talk to her. He'd find someplace quiet and he'd use reason. He'd confess to his growing feelings for her. He could not let someone as good as she was slip through his fingers.

He would win her back.

WILLA WISHED SHE had never married Matt. Or let down her guard.

Men seemed to come in only one mold. Her instincts had been right about him.

Well, he had her fortune, but he didn't have her.

But where would she go?

And that was when she noticed her mother coming out of the card room and into the ballroom. She walked up to her. "I wish to go home," Willa said.

Her mother blinked at the lack of preamble or greeting. "Where is your husband?"

"I don't know," Willa lied. "However, I have taken ill." That was a truth. She didn't know what would happen if she stayed at this event much longer.

And then she caught sight of Camberly coming around the corner. She wrapped her arm around her mother's and steered her toward the ballroom. "Please, Mother, take me home."

With concerned eyes, her mother placed her hand over Willa's. Willa wanted to scream at her to *go*. Instead, her mother asked quietly, "What is it?"

"I married a man like Father." Did she understand? Out of consideration for her mother's feelings, Willa had never openly expressed herself.

Camberly came up behind them. "Willa—"

"My daughter is not feeling well, Your Grace," her mother said with surprising strength. "I'm certain you understand." She didn't wait for his response but took Willa's arm and guided her into the ballroom and toward the front hallway and the door. Willa kept her head down, not wanting to see *him*, or anyone.

Camberly trailed after them. "I shall see her home."

Her mother stopped, turned to him. "*Please*, Your Grace."

For a second, he appeared helpless. "I need to explain."

"*Tomorrow*," her mother said.

Willa sensed his struggle with her mother's edict, and then in a hollow voice, he said, "Shall I see that your coach is brought around?"

"That would be kind. Thank you."

When there was no further comment, Willa asked, afraid to look around, "Is he gone?"

"He has left," her mother said.

Willa straightened. "I take it Father is not here."

"I have not seen him." Her mother sounded very tired.

As they made their way to the door, their hostess, Lady Evanston, caught up with them. "I'm so sorry to hear Her Grace is not feeling well."

"It is unfortunate, my lady," her mother said. "However, we've enjoyed this evening. Your decorations are truly amazing. Everyone will be talking about this ball for years to come."

"Yes, I'm rather proud of myself. Is your husband here, Mrs. Reverly? Does he know you are leaving?"

"He is here . . . somewhere," Willa's mother answered. "I have not had the opportunity to tell him of my plans. Will you do so when you see him? I will send the coach back for him."

"Of course," Her Ladyship said. "Please, Your Grace, let us know how you are faring on the morrow. Can you believe Camberly? He is beside himself with worry."

"Such a gentleman," her mother agreed. In a low voice to Willa, she said, "Just a few more steps and we can be free."

Willa trusted her mother to guide her.

In the main hall, the duke waited for them by the door. "Your coach is here." He walked out the door with them. "May I see you at home?" he asked Willa.

Her response was to turn her face even more into her mother's shoulder.

"How generous of you, Your Grace. However, I believe it best we quarantine my daughter. You do understand?"

There was a long pause. Willa struggled with a strong desire to speak for herself. To hurl words at him.

He answered, "Very well. I will do as my wife wishes."

And then Willa was angry that he hadn't protested, that he'd been so agreeable.

But she kept silent. She wasn't about to spare him so much as a glance. He was free now to pursue Letty all night or any of the other ladies who had been eyeing him this evening.

As they were leaving the house, Willa overheard one woman whisper to another about what a gentleman the duke was for the way he was concerned about his wife. "So kind. So caring."

"How fortunate for her," was the answer.

Willa practically ran down the Evanston steps. She climbed inside her family's coach.

Her mother paused to tell their driver, Lloyd, to drive until she gave the word where she wished to go next.

"Yes, ma'am."

She joined Willa in the coach and he shut the door.

"I'm destroyed—" Willa started, but her mother shut her off with one raised finger.

She leaned out the window and waved at Lady Collins and several of her other friends who had gathered on the step with Lady Evanston. They waved back, and then put their heads together to gossip.

Her mother sat back. "Voices carry in the night. 'Overheard' gossip is the best sort."

"Perhaps we need new friends. And new husbands."

Cool gray eyes surveyed her as if she was an obstinate child. "What happened?"

"I found him with Letty Bainhurst."

Her mother sighed her relief.

"You act almost happy with the news," Willa said with reproach.

"I knew the whispers about his uncle and, well, one never knows."

"His uncle? The one who died? What are you talking about?"

"Let us say, his uncle William was not fond of women."

Willa frowned and then started when she realized what her mother was implying. "But that is not Matt. Not him at all."

"Good," her mother answered, and then she shrugged. "Catching the duke with Letty is not such a big matter."

"It is to me."

"Men will be who they are." She spoke as if by rote. "Even if he had been of the same mind as his uncle, I would say what I am about to say—Willa, you will return to your husband. We will drive around a bit and then I will take you to his home."

"You might as well take me there now," Willa answered. "I can see you are not going to understand."

"I can see that my daughter is hopelessly naïve."

"Because I believe marriage vows are to be honored," she flashed back. "He said he would be faithful. And I am not like you."

There was a long beat of silence between them, and then her mother asked coolly, "What does that mean?"

For a moment, Willa wished she hadn't broached the subject, and then she said, "I can't pretend to be happy, that all is well . . . when it isn't."

"You are in *love*," her mother accused her.

"Isn't that how it is supposed to be?"

"For a duchess? No. Not even for a rich man's daughter. Why should you be more fortunate than the rest of us? Or believe you have higher expectations?"

Willa faced her mother. "Because I want it *all*. And, to be honest, I was starting to believe I did."

"What is 'all'?"

"A husband who doesn't disappear whenever I need him. Who cherishes me and acts as if he enjoys my company." Matt had almost convinced her both of those things were true. Of course, this morning by the river, she'd had her first brush with the truth. "I want to believe that I matter to someone." She'd wanted to matter to *him*.

"You matter, Willa. You are a duchess. His duchess. A woman can ask for no more in life."

"I can. I don't want to be a blank piece of paper."

"What does that mean?"

"It means I won't settle. Not in love. Or in how I live my life."

"Your father and I have provided well for you."

"You have. But you have also kept me on a shelf, waiting for the right time to marry me off at a good advantage."

Her mother compressed her lips in a tight, hard line. The sound of the coach wheels over cobblestones filled the silence between them. They were not far from home. The horses had picked up their pace.

And then, her mother reached for the speaker tube between passenger and driver. "Take us to the Duke of Camberly's." Her mother sat back in the seat.

Willa's hands clenched into fists. "You are returning me to him? Even though I don't wish to go?"

"You won't discover if you truly matter to him hiding in your childhood bed," her mother answered. "You must face him."

"I don't know if I wish to. What do I say?"

"What you just told me. You were very articulate."

"But it is harder speaking to him that way."

"Then you are lying to yourself. Willa, people don't just hand over what you want. You take it. Not speaking to Camberly will lead you nowhere. I know." Her mother was quiet a moment before saying, "You believe I don't care what your father does—"

"He is selfish, how can you tolerate him?"

"Because I love him," her mother answered. "Because in spite of what he does and who he is, I wish to think that someday, there will be something meaningful between us. And also because I have few other choices. You see, I hid from your father instead of speaking my truth. I can't say that if I had done things differently, we might be different. He is a hard man, and a frightened one. He's afraid of being poor, of aging, of being overlooked. But I'm at peace with that. I was the one who didn't believe I had a right to make demands. I was silly." She turned to look at the passing scenery. "Don't you be silly, Willa. You've told Camberly how you feel. Now you owe it to yourself to hear him out."

The coach rolled to a stop. The ever-vigilant Marshall opened the house door to welcome her home.

Willa reached for her mother's hand. "What if I truly don't matter to my husband?"

"Then you are in no different a place than where you are right now, except he does care. I saw his face."

"But does he care enough to love *me*?"

"Possibly. And I'm jealous. Now go on. A good night's sleep will do wonders."

Sleep was always her mother's answer to all the trials of life. There had been a time when Willa had wanted to scream when she heard her mother say it.

Now, she kissed her mother's cheek. "Thank you."

Her mother smiled, but then a thoughtful look crossed her face. "How did you know to search for Camberly?"

"Lady Evanston told me that my husband wished me to go to that room. She said he had a surprise for me."

"Letty could have arranged all of this."

"It is possible," Willa conceded. "She seemed very pleased with herself."

"Give him a chance to explain, Willa. Hear him out."

"I will." It would be difficult . . . but she would try to listen to her husband, even if she didn't believe him.

And then? Well, Willa knew she'd have a decision to make. A hard one.

At a nod from her mother, Lloyd opened the coach door and Willa climbed out. Thoughtfully, she walked to where Marshall waited. She told him good night and made her way up the stairs.

Annie was waiting up for her. The maid had been sitting in the desk chair by the lamp doing some handwork. At the sight of Willa, Annie set her work aside and jumped to her feet. "How was your evening, Your Grace?" she asked hopefully.

"Trying."

"Is His Grace with you?"

"He'll be along shortly." Willa looked to the bed. It looked empty without him, as would her life.

She felt her throat start to close and the burn of tears. She blinked them back. It was never good to cry in front of Annie. She always wished to right every wrong, and this was between Willa and Matt.

Nor was Willa ready for a confrontation with him. It might be best to wait for the morning. As Annie pulled the pins from her hair, Willa decided she would prefer being in bed and pretending sleep. Let Matt make the first move. After all, she was the wronged party.

Consequently, Willa had little patience with the rituals of brushing out her hair and braiding it. He could arrive home at any moment.

She knew Annie's mind buzzed with questions. Thankfully, the maid knew enough not to ask.

This night, Willa chose her heaviest nightdress to wear—another sign to Matt that, although she'd decided to return to their home, she was not pleased. "Thank you, Annie. You have been most helpful."

"I try to do my best, Miss Willa. Do you wish to keep the light burning for His Grace?"

"No." Darkness was good.

"Yes, Your Grace. Have sweet dreams."

Yes, Willa would dream about a man who loved her and her alone.

The sourness of her thoughts disturbed her . . . because, she realized, she did love Matt, and him alone. No matter what happened.

That was her last thought before surprising herself by falling asleep, but not for long.

One moment she'd laid her head upon the pillow; in the next, someone stuffed a ball of material in her mouth and tied a scarf around her head to prevent her from crying out. Confused, her eyes opened in surprise to realize the room was still dark. That was her last thought before a pillowcase was tossed over her head.

Rough hands grabbed her by the arms, pulled her from the bed, and bound her with ropes.

Willa found herself hoisted up on a man's shoulder and being carried from her room.

Chapter 12

Watching the Reverly coach pulling away, Matt felt as if he was in a madman's play.

In less than an hour, his life had been upended. Willa's accusations stung . . . because there had been an element of truth to them.

And he believed he was on the verge of losing someone who could be very special to him.

Letty had appealed to the part of him that wanted to be heroic. He'd pictured himself as saving her from a horrid marriage.

Instead, watching his wife being driven away, he now pictured himself as an adulterer. An ugly word. Certainly not a heroic one.

As the son of a man who had given up his birthright for the woman he loved, as the brother of sisters who were happily married to good, honest men, Matt felt shame.

He had slept with another man's wife, and he'd justified doing so in his mind because Letty hadn't loved her husband.

Standing among the glittering company of the *ton*, Matt felt a fraud. This was not the man he wanted to be. Worse, his weakness had enabled Hardesty to manipulate him.

He pulled the note Letty had given him from his pocket. Hardesty had plotted the meeting. He wouldn't have put it past the man to have arranged for Willa to come upon them.

Matt needed more answers, and the best person to give them to him was Letty. He returned to the ballroom to seek her out. He also wanted to seek out the Minotaur footman who had delivered the note to him, and ask a few questions.

Letty was nowhere to be found. He searched all the rooms, however, it was as if she had vanished.

He was stumped.

"You look so lonely, Your Grace," Lady Evanston's voice said behind him. There was a hint of invitation in her tone.

He confronted his hostess, a smile fixed firmly on his face. "I'm not."

Her lower lip curled. "That is unfortunate. However, if you ever do feel you need company, think of me." As she moved past him, she reached for his gloved hand and pressed a folded note into it. She didn't pause but kept walking.

The paper was the same sort that Hardesty had used. Lady Evanston had written, *See me upstairs, first floor, third door, right after midnight.* The handwriting was different.

He went after her. Before she could go too far, he caught her arm.

She acted pleased that he'd given chase, until he said, "Where did you write this note?"

"What note?" she asked brightly, and looked around as if checking to see if someone overheard them. Matt was having none of it.

"This paper, where did you find it?"

Lady Evanston's frown said that wasn't what she'd expected him to say. Nor did she appear pleased he was waving her invitation around in such a public forum.

He kept his voice quiet and carefully neutral. "I need to know, and if you don't tell me, then I shall ask your husband."

Her chin lifted. "Richard doesn't care."

"I am not concerned if he cares or not. I want to know where you keep this paper."

"In the study."

"Take me to it."

The light of interest returned to her eye as if she was imagining he was playing some lover's game. "What is in it for me, Your Grace?"

Matt wanted to answer that doing so would mean he didn't throttle her, but that would have been an empty threat. One couldn't throttle ladies in their own ballrooms, more's the pity. "We shall see, won't we?" he answered with his own touch of flirtation.

She couldn't do enough for him then. "Meet me at the hall door, by the card room. Five minutes."

"And the study is where?"

Lady Evanston made an impatient sound. "Down the side hall. Five minutes," she repeated, and charged off into the crowd.

Matt had no intention of following. The study was obviously the name for the sitting room where he'd met Letty. Anyone could have gone there to write notes.

Hardesty was at this party.

He studied the faces in the crowd. Would Hardesty be as old as his grandfather? Or much younger?

What did a blackmailer look like? What was the face of a thief?

And he was playing a fool's game, he realized.

In time, Hardesty would let him know what he wanted. All Matt had to do was stay vigilant.

"Your Grace, we are so happy to have a moment of your time," a matronly woman in a red velvet turban said. She was accompanied by several other ladies of her same generation.

"I'm happy to be present for you," Matt said, perfunctorily. His mind was on determining his next step.

"I'm Lady Ralston and these are my friends Dame Honora and Mrs. Simpkins. We are presiding members of the Mayfair Literary Society."

"How nice for you," Matt said.

"We are hoping you would agree to read for us from your book *Love Fulfilled* at our next meeting. We are proud to have a copy."

Matt swallowed a sound of frustration. This was the second time today that his very bad poetry had been mentioned. He did his best to tell them no in a polite way and made his escape. He knew if they cornered Minerva, he might have to honor their request—but he was not going to agree easily.

He was also beginning to realize how fruitless it was for him to search for Hardesty, a person he knew nothing about. He could quiz the servants, but he would have to go through all the footmen, since he had no idea which Minotaur had delivered the note.

Ready to leave the Evanston rout, he searched out his grandmother. Minerva was surrounded by friends. When he suggested they leave, she informed him she was enjoying herself.

"Then may I leave?" Matt was not in the mood to wait. He needed to talk to Willa.

"Go on, go on," Minerva said. "But send back the coach. I promised Lady Cahill a ride home."

"You may have it. I'll walk." The distance was not far. "Also, if presiding members of the Mayfair Literary Society approach you, tell them I don't do readings."

"I will," was the breezy reply.

Given permission to go, Matt didn't say his good-byes to his host and hostess. Diana Evanston was presumably in the study waiting for him, and Matt had no desire to look her husband in the eye. He set his hat on his head and left the house.

The night air was cool. The considerable traffic on the street grew sparser the closer he traveled to home. Matt wasn't one for the affectation of a walking stick. He passed several gentlemen carrying theirs. They twirled them, and several saluted him with them. A few acted as if they wished to engage him in conversation. Matt kept walking, his mind working on what he would say to Willa. What he *wanted* to say.

He turned the corner onto his street. Lamps burned by his front door. He prayed Willa was home. Since she'd left with her mother, she might not be.

And that would be the test, wouldn't it? If Willa chose to return to his home, then there was a strong chance for them. If she hadn't—?

Then he'd find her. And he would make her listen to him—

A thickset man stepped out from the shadows. He wore a heavy coat on such a pleasant autumn evening and a hat pulled low over his eyes.

"The Duke of Camberly?"

Matt stopped. Since he was taller than most men, few ever picked fights with him. He also knew how to hold his own. "What do you want?"

"Mr. Hardesty sent me," the man said. He slurred his words the way those born around the docks spoke.

Curling his gloved hands into fists, Matt asked carefully, "What does Hardesty want?"

The man reached inside his coat.

Matt half expected him to hand over another folded note. He thought about overpowering the man and dragging his carcass to his house. There, he'd do what he must to squeeze information about Hardesty out of him.

But the man surprised him. Instead of a note, he held his fingers out as if they had ahold of something. Matt couldn't make it out in the dark.

"Go on, take it," the man said.

Matt held out his gloved hand. The man dropped a thick curl of rich brown hair into his palm. "Your wife wants you to come with me. If you don't, she will be sorry."

"What have you done?"

"This way to find out, Your Grace."

"I'm not going with you anywhere until I know she is all right." Because if she wasn't, Matt was going to murder the man.

"Oh, she is fine—for now. Lovely thing she is, Your Grace. A tasty bit. Mr. Hardesty has buyers for her. He hoped you would listen to reason but if not, there won't be any slack for us."

Matt closed his hand over the curl. He wanted to pound the man into the ground. "How did you take her?"

The blackguard grinned. He was missing two front teeth. Matt had an urge to knock the rest of his teeth down his throat. "We nabbed her from her bed, right there in your big house. We are so good, no one even knows she is gone, except you and me. Are you coming, Your Grace? Or is she mine?"

So Willa had come home to him. She'd been waiting for him.

Or the man was lying.

"You tell Hardesty he's a bastard."

"You can tell him yourself, Your Grace. But first, you must come with me."

"Lead the way." Matt could be walking into a trap . . . but his every instinct said the man was speaking the truth. Hardesty had Willa.

He followed the brute back behind the houses to an alley. Two small horses were tied up there. "Take your pick, Your Grace." He was growing cocky. Matt would relish the moment when he changed the tables on them.

His horse groaned when he climbed on top of it. The saddle was too small, and Matt had to let down the stirrups.

"Be careful with my animal," the man ordered. "I value that horse."

"As much as you value my wife's life?" Matt didn't hide his disdain.

"I don't give a rat's ass what becomes of her, Your Grace. I'm paid to do a job, and I do it."

On those words, Hardesty's man put his heel to horse, and off he went. If Matt believed Willa was in their clutches, then he'd best follow.

He followed.

WILLA'S ASSAILANTS HAD bound her arms, wrists, and legs, and had carried her out of her house as if she was little more than a rug. She'd tried to struggle, but she'd been overpowered.

No one had stopped them. No cry had gone up. They'd taken the servants' entrance and then carried her through the back garden. She'd heard the back gate open right before they'd thrown her onto the floor of what seemed to be a post chaise.

Then they had cut a piece of her hair.

"Ross, you know where to meet me?" one of them had asked. He sounded like one of the dockworkers.

The other man had answered, "Aye, Donel, I know." Willa had listened for clues. She now knew Ross was Irish. Donel was their leader. They had known the layout of the house.

There came the snap of reins, and the chaise began moving with her on the floor inside.

The ride had been uncomfortable. She hated the gag and swore to herself that once she could spit it out, she'd give her captors a tongue lashing they would not forget.

But first, she had to free herself.

She squirmed and twisted, her efforts making her bonds tighter. She changed her focus. Her goal became the liberation of one finger, then two. It took concentration and a patience her fear threatened to overthrow.

Minutes seemed like hours as she worked, and then, to her surprise, she managed, with a great deal of pain and effort, to slide her right thumb underneath one of the rough ropes.

It gave her hope, and she set to work to free her index finger.

And when she escaped her bonds? What would she do then? She didn't know.

She couldn't even understand their game. Did they plan to hold her for ransom? A few months ago, the papers had stories of a young woman abducted from her home. She was never seen or heard from again, even though her family had searched and searched.

Could it be that these men were the ones who had taken the hapless woman? And were they now intent on treating Willa to what they'd done to her?

She tried not to think too deeply on the subject because it did make her afraid, and right now, she needed all the courage she could muster.

The saddest part was that Matt would come home and not find her in their bed. He'd think she had stayed with her mother. He'd never know that she had come home until it was too late.

The wheels of the vehicle went off the main road. By the way they bounced, they seemed to be on little more than a cow path. Willa hated the rough ride. It was all she could do to protect herself. To her amazement, she managed to slip her index finger loose from her bonds.

The chaise came to a halt. Ross jumped down from the driver's seat, and a door opened near Willa's head. She lay still as if she slept and prayed he could not see her hands.

But he was not interested in her hands.

"You are a pretty morsel," he said. A hand explored her body over her nightdress. There was a chill in the air, but she didn't shiver from the cold.

His hand squeezed her breast. "I don't know how much time we have. I'd like a bit of you. Even a taste." He laughed, the sound without mirth. "Pity what's going to happen to you." He gave her breast another squeeze, and then there was the sound of riders.

The door was shut.

God help her.

She thought of Matt. And how she would never have the chance to tell him that he had won her heart. She'd never be able to feel his warmth around her. Or hear his voice—

"Dismount, Your Grace," she heard Donel say.

"Where is she? I must know my wife is all right before I do another word you say."

Matt. Her heart leaped with joy, and then froze with fear. They used her to control him.

Her mind screamed at him to run.

The door opened again. "She's right here," Ross said. He pulled the pillowcase from her head. A light was held up. Willa went still, keeping her eyes closed because she didn't want them to see her fear.

"Release her," Matt ordered. "Let her go and then I will do whatever you wish. Tell Hardesty he has my word on it."

"You are going to do whatever we wish anyway, Your Grace," Donel said. "Ross, hold that cudgel over the girl's head, and if he does anything he shouldn't, bash her brains in."

"Aye," came the answer.

Hot tears pressed against Willa's eyelids. They were going to kill them both. Together.

She heard Matt dismount. In a cold voice, he said, "What would you have me do now?"

No, Willa wanted to scream. They were going to kill her no matter what.

"Ross, tie him up and put him with his lady."

In a matter of minutes, Matt's body was dumped on the floor beside Willa. They pushed her against the seat base as if she was nothing more than a sack of grain, her back to her husband's. His legs were too long for the width of the vehicle, so Donel and Ross had to double him up. Willa felt very squeezed.

"What now?" Ross wondered.

"Now we drown them. Hardesty wants a coaching accident."

Ross swore. "Why can't we just kill them and be done? It's work to make deaths look like accidents."

"Oh, well, you can give Hardesty your suggestions yourself. As for me, I'm being paid to drown them."

"How are we doing that?"

"Drive the vehicle into the river. We'll make it appear as if they attempted a shortcut to the main road but drove off."

"And why were they out here?" Ross said. "And why wouldn't he be riding in his own coach? He's a bloody duke."

Donel did not like the questions. "If he had come home in his coach, I would have used it. But don't tell me dukes don't hire chaises. They do."

"Yes, but why are they out here?"

"I asked the same question," Donel said. "Hardesty said not to worry. He'd have a story. He wanted them drowned along this road. It is a shortcut to somewhere."

Willa knew where they were going to be taken. There was a shorter route to Mayfield that did follow two tracks along the River Lea, the same river where they had been fishing earlier. No one would question their being there.

"He always has a story. It's easier to just break necks. Nice and clean. But it is sad. She is a sweet thing," Ross said with regret. He sighed. "All right then, what is the plan?"

Willa strained to hear the tale—

Two fingers clasped hers.

She started, thankful she had a gag, or she would have made a sound in surprise. His thumb felt for her ropes. His hands were larger and stronger. He tried to slip his finger under her ropes. They were too tight, but she could slip her free fingers under his. She might be able to free him.

She pulled, while he twisted and yanked on his hand.

Meanwhile, Ross and Donel discussed the "plan."

"We are going to tip the coach into the Lea? Horse and all? That horse won't stand for it," Ross protested.

"We'll shoot the horse," Donel answered.

"The hell we will. I'll not be party to killing a horse. Donel, you can't ask that of me."

"And how do we make it appear a coaching accident if the horse is free?"

"He escaped." Ross spoke as if the answer was simple. "Animals are smart. He freed himself from his traces and swam to shore."

"He freed himself?"

"It could happen. Listen, that horse is worth money. We sell it, we make a bit more."

There was a beat of silence. "Aye," Donel agreed. "You can sell it."

"I know a man."

"All right. Fine."

Willa found one of the knots in Matt's bindings and, using thumb and index finger, frantically tried to untie it.

"All right, but before we loose the horse, drive the chaise right up to the edge of the bank," Donel said. "Then you have your horse and we will push the chaise into the river."

"Are we going to untie them? Won't look like much of an accident if they are all bound up."

"I will cut their bonds after they drown. The coach will keep them from floating away until we finish."

"I'm not going to help you with all that. I don't fiddle with the bodies. Not after they are dead."

"You are such a lass," Donel mocked him.

"I don't like it."

"I *know*. You can murder them but you don't like touching them afterwards. You are a puss—"

There was the sound of flesh hitting flesh. Of male grunts and half-finished swearing.

Willa hoped they killed each other.

A body was slammed against the coach and then yanked away. Donel growled before saying, "Don't touch me again, or I swear, I'll throw you into that vehicle with them. Now help me drag this chaise to the water."

Ross didn't offer any protest.

The chaise began moving. Panicked, Willa worked the knot.

The horse grew nervous and balked. Ross swore while Donel shouted orders. "Make sure we are as close to the bank as possible. We are going to pitch it in on its side as if it fell over."

The coach moved forward a few feet. Matt tugged on her ropes. *Don't do that*, Willa silently warned him. That was how she'd made hers so tight, and then she realized he had one hand free—

"We need to cut the horse loose, Donel. There is no sense to this. He's skittish."

Choice words were Donel's answer, and then there was the sound of racing hooves. "I thought you had him, Ross?"

"I can't see what you are doing. It's black as hell here. The damn beast bolted before I could hold him."

"You can go after him as soon as we push this chaise in," Donel said. "Come, give me a hand. I want this done."

The chaise began to rock in one direction and then fell back. "Put more into it," Donel snapped.

"I need to chase that horse before someone else nabs him."

"The coach first. Come over here. Heave to. One, two, three—"

The chaise tilted. For the span of a heartbeat, it seemed to hold itself up by two wheels, and then it was falling into the water.

Chapter 13

$\mathcal{W}$ith Willa's help, Matt had one hand free and he managed to slip the other from the ropes just as the chaise hit the water.

His and Willa's bodies tumbled over each other. Water poured in through the windows and any cracks in the hired vehicle. Three quarters of the chaise's cab filled with cold water—and then it hit the riverbed and stopped.

Thank God.

He reached out, catching Willa with one arm and lifting her out of the water so she could breathe. The knot in her gag was wet, and the cold river water made his hands clumsy. He attempted to pull the cloth up and succeeded in lifting it over her head. He yanked the wet gag from her mouth. She took a huge, sputtering breath, her chest heaving as if her lungs couldn't take in enough air. He covered her mouth with his hand, warning her to silence.

"Keep your head above water," he whispered.

She nodded, her body going into a spasm of shaking, but she controlled herself as best she could.

"That's my girl," he answered. Both of their legs were bound but he could stand propped against the chaise and she rested on his body. The river's current was swift. There was enough water to send the chaise floating if they weren't careful. The vehicle rocked slightly as he started trying to untie Willa's hands.

On the bank, Ross asked, "Did you know it was shallow here?"

"I did. You think I'm going to swim out to cut them free?"

"I'm going for the horse. I don't want him to run too far."

"Go on," Donel answered.

"Don't enjoy yourself too much," Ross called. Matt thought of Donel's knife.

"I'll meet you at the Blue Boar," was the barked reply. There was the sound of a horse riding off. Donel would be coming.

The inside of the chaise was ink black. It rested on its side, the door over Matt's head. He lifted Willa the best he could with one arm to keep her head above the water, while he prepared for that door to open—and yet, when it did, Matt felt his heart give a start.

A human-shaped head was silhouetted against the night sky. Donel couldn't see anything inside the coach. It was impossible.

Matt punched upward with all his might.

He struck the man square in the face. Donel lost balance and fell backward into the water.

Overjoyed by his good luck, Matt took hold of Willa by the back of her nightdress. He grabbed the side of the door and attempted to pull his big body out of the coach. His bound legs were a hindrance, as was Willa's weight, even as slight as she was. When he had an arm and elbow outside the coach, he thought to raise Willa up first—

A fist came down on Matt's head. A flash of stars momentarily blinded his vision. Donel then gripped Matt by the hair to jerk his head back for another blow.

However, Matt was the larger man. He was hampered by his hold on Willa, but he refused to let go of her. Instead, he released his hold on the coach, blindly reaching for Donel. His hand found material, and Matt allowed his weight to fall, dragging the bastard into the cab after him.

Now it was Donel who was thrown off as he landed headfirst into the water swirling up to Matt's waist. Donel tried to rise, to find his footing.

Fury took hold of Matt. He was fighting for both his and Willa's lives. It was as if he had the strength of ten men. He used his elbow to smash Donel's head against the wall.

Donel cried out at the blow, but before he could react, Matt shoved him under the water again. This time, Matt was not going to let him up.

He was also determined to push Willa out the door. He wasn't gentle. He couldn't afford to be. Donel had grabbed Matt's legs and was trying to topple him. However, Willa had blessedly managed to free one hand and, with a boost from Matt, pulled herself out of the coach.

Believing her safe, Matt gave his full attention to his attacker. He brought his hands down, capping the top of Donel's head.

Matt had the advantage of being taller and more muscular but Donel was a cunning fighter who had his own good amount of strength. He tried to bite Matt's thigh to make him let go. Matt just pushed him deeper.

The interior of the coach was as black as Hades. Donel's hands were like claws. He was struggling for breath now, and still Matt held him down.

He thought of Donel's wicked knife. He didn't know why the man wasn't using it.

Donel tried to roll away from him. Matt would not let him escape. If Matt didn't stop him, Donel would harm Willa. Donel's hands began to flail. Bubbles rose from him as if he could hold his breath no longer.

Matt pushed him deeper, using his superior strength—

And then the struggle was over.

The fight was gone. Donel's body sank.

Matt had to forcibly pull his hands back. He was trembling from the exertion, the fear, the misery of what he'd just done.

Exhausted, he fell back against the side of the coach, the movement shifting the vehicle.

"*Matt,*" Willa shouted, followed by a splash.

Alarmed, Matt reached for the door above him. His muscles quivered from the exertion. There was the sound of more splashing. He roared his frustration and found the extra effort he needed to lift himself out. He flopped into the water, his legs still bound.

Willa was right beside the coach. He raised her up. His feet found the riverbed and he braced her against him. She coughed, hacking up water—and then curled into him, shivering.

At first, he thought she was crying. Dear God, she was alive. They both were.

She raised her head. Her eyes had an unholy gleam in the moonlight. "Is he dead?"

"He's dead."

"Good. May we go to shore?"

"We may."

The problem was making their way there. Matt hopped and kicked like a fish to see them to safety. He placed Willa on the bank among the weeds and rushes. His hand hit something metal—Donel's knife. He must have lost it when he cut the horse loose. Matt now used it to cut the ropes on his legs.

Willa had tried to drag herself higher up the bank. The sky was lightening. The paleness of her nightdress was now a muddy gray. Her bedraggled braid was like a black rope over her shoulder.

"Here," Matt said, to gain her attention.

She looked to him and he climbed the last bit of the bank to her and began sawing at her ropes. One wrist was still bound to a rope around her waist. She'd torn her nails in trying to save herself, and him.

Willa cried out as he cut the ropes on her ankles. They had been far too tight. "It is like a thousand needles."

"Take it easy," he whispered, lightly rubbing her ankles and bare feet to help ease her pain. She appeared to shake her head as if in answer until he realized she was shaking uncontrollably and the tremors were growing stronger. But she was alive—

Matt kissed her.

He placed his hands on either side of her face and pressed his lips to hers. Her arms came around him. She pressed herself close as if she could climb right into his skin, and he wanted her there.

Their kiss said more than words. They were both all right. They were alive. *He'd killed a man*, but he'd had no choice. No choice.

And it had been harder than one would have thought. Drowning the life force out of another human had called for everything he had.

The kiss grew harder, more urgent, but not sexual.

In this kiss, he released his horror for what he'd done, and she answered. She understood. She knew his pain. He'd had no choice.

He pulled her into his lap, their lips never breaking contact, and she breathed life back into him.

She restored his soul.

Matt broke the kiss. "I'm sorry. So sorry." Her arms were around his neck.

"It wasn't your fault."

She was right, and yet—

"If not for me, you would not have been in danger," Matt said. "I'll find the bastard Hardesty." And then, memory returned. "Willa, there is nothing between Letty and me. Please, trust me. I was tricked into going there."

Her answer was a half-crazed laugh. "How can you worry about that right now?" She placed her hands on his cheeks and lifted his head to look into his eyes. "I'm just grateful you are alive. They wanted us dead, Matt."

"Yes." Anger rose as a wave inside him. And the need for vengeance. He wanted blood.

But first, he must take care of his wife.

She was shaking again. She was naked under the nightdress, her feet bare.

"How are your wrists and ankles?"

"Better," she answered. He shrugged off his jacket, the one he'd worn to the Evanston party. The sleeves were torn at the shoulder seam and it wasn't easy removing the wet material, but he managed.

He wrapped his jacket around her. "I'm sorry I don't have anything dry but this should help." She nodded, bending her knees and pulling her feet close to her as she seemingly disappeared in the coat.

"Stay here," he warned. There were things he must do to finish this night's business.

He waded back into the water toward the coach. He was in stocking feet; the river mud had sucked away his evening shoes. He climbed back inside and lifted Donel's body up. It took a good amount of effort, but he managed to drag it out of the coach and then roll it into the water.

"What are you doing?" Willa asked from shore, her voice carrying in the stillness.

He let Donel go in deeper water, and the man floated away.

"What did you do?" Willa demanded as he splashed back to shore.

Matt climbed the bank before answering. "I didn't want anyone to find him or associate him with the chaise."

"Why not?"

"It seemed prudent."

She studied him a moment. "You aren't going to tell the authorities about this, are you?"

"No." One of the horses was still tied and waiting. He walked over to it. Matt was shaking as well from the night air and the aftermath of what he'd done. He led the horse to Willa.

"Why aren't you going to report what happened?" she wanted to know. "Those men tried to kill us." Her spirit was returning. "One is still free."

"I know." He picked up the knife.

"We should have the magistrate storm the Blue Boar."

"We should," he agreed, not sharing his true thoughts.

"Let's go then," she said. She was still shivering but she came to her feet. He needed to see her safe before she caught her death.

Before they both did.

He mounted and then reached for her hand to pull her up in front of him in the saddle. She settled in to him. He sent the horse forward.

"Matt, what is this about?" she asked. "It can't be about blackmail. Not any longer."

"No. Whoever is behind this wants more than money." He told her all, needing to go through it in his own mind. He spoke of blackmail and of William's secret, and of Minerva's belief her oldest son had been murdered. Of the notes at the ball that were still in his pocket and probably hopelessly ruined.

Willa listened.

Matt knew he should not involve her in this. As if reading his mind, she prodded, "Matt, they took me from our bed. They knew the floor plan of the house."

"You came home to me." It was as he had hoped, and it had almost cost her life.

She looked up at him. "I didn't come home to you, Matt. I came home to *us*."

He kissed her head. Yes, *us*.

However, his wife's practical mind was working. "Matt, why would Hardesty move on to murder?"

"That is what I'm wondering. If I'm dead, I can't pay him anything."

"And there must be a purpose to his scheme tonight. I feel quite strongly that he wished to separate us this evening." She puzzled on the matter before asking, "You've never heard of or met a Hardesty before?"

"Never. I've even thought about school friends. No one. But I am starting to believe that Hardesty is a false name."

She leaned her head against his chest. "Then he could be anyone."

"No, not anyone. Someone who stands to gain if I die." And Matt suddenly had an idea, one that was hard to contemplate. However, as he considered it, possibilities fell into place.

It was a betrayal. He would need proof before he accepted it . . . such as meeting Ross at the Blue Boar.

Whatever money Hardesty paid the villain, Matt would pay more.

Matt looked at the sky. Dawn was near.

They reached the main road. It was busy with the usual traffic flowing into the city in the very wee hours of the morning. People walked among ox and dog carts, wagons loaded with vegetables for London tables and fodder for horses. Everyone was too busy to notice anything unusual about them.

He rode straight to his house. Here, the hour was too early for anyone to notice them. As he pulled the horse up, the front door opened and a harried Marshall ran out.

"Good morning, Your Grace." He sounded his usual self except anxious eyes took in Matt and Willa's shabby, damp appearances. "We have been most worried since we found the duchess missing."

"As you should have been," Matt said.

"We did not share this information with the dowager," Marshall added.

"Quite wise." Matt dismounted and then took Willa in his arms. "Have a hot bath prepared immediately for the duchess." He didn't wait for his orders to be obeyed but carried his wife into the house and up the stairs.

Her complexion was almost bloodless. She clutched his shirt with one hand.

Annie waited anxiously in their room, and then almost fell back in horror when she saw Willa in her nightdress caked with mud and damp, and both of them smelling of the river. "Your Grace, I am relieved to see you."

"As we are to be here. A bath is coming for your mistress. Meanwhile, fetch the brandy and two glasses." Annie hurried to obey.

"You can set me down," Willa said. "I'm not that fragile." She was shaking again.

"Perhaps I like holding you."

Her response was to rest her head against his shoulder. "We are most fortunate."

He grimly nodded.

Annie brought brandy. Matt would have happily kept Willa in his lap but she insisted on moving to the chair across from his at the desk. He poured two healthy glasses. "Drink." He set her glass in front of her and she took a sip.

He understood the restorative power of brandy. He drained his to show her how it was done.

Willa frowned. "I don't like it that much."

He smiled. "You are feeling more yourself."

"Why? Because I'm arguing with you?"

He let his smile be his answer.

Matt stood up and crossed to the washbasin. The water was hot. He could have blessed Annie. He washed his face and his hands, all the while keeping a watchful eye on Willa as she sipped more of the brandy. Color was now returning to her cheeks.

Footmen appeared with the bath. Annie set up the privacy screen so that Matt and Willa were blocked from their view. "She thinks of everything," Matt murmured.

Willa heard him and nodded. However, he now had a new idea. After the footmen had left, Matt sought a quiet moment with Annie. "Are there servants or workmen around this house who go by the names of Ross or Donel?"

"Is Ross Irish?"

"Yes."

Anne nodded. "There is a stableman named Ross. He is not in your employ."

"Has he been in the house?" Willa asked.

"A time or two. Cook is sweet on him. Mrs. Snow is partial to him as well. You know how the Irish are. We can work with anyone, Your Grace."

"Thank you, Annie," Willa answered. "Would you leave us now?"

The maid bobbed a curtsey and left the room. "Well," Willa said, "we now know why Ross knew his way around the house."

"Shall I have a conversation with Mrs. Snow and Cook, or should you?"

"Marshall should," she said.

She was right.

Willa took off the fouled nightdress and climbed into the tub. She washed the river off her body, then it was his turn. He'd shaved while she'd bathed.

"I'm exhausted," Willa said.

Matt nodded, not wanting her to know what he planned.

She put on a clean gown. "A few hours' sleep, and then we must speak to someone. We must report what happened."

Yes, he wanted her to sleep.

No, he was not going to wait. He could not relax with Ross free to run.

"Have you ever heard of the Blue Boar?" Willa asked. She got into bed.

As a matter of fact, he had. Most gentlemen knew the whoring hell called the Blue Boar. "No."

She'd be furious that he lied. It might even spark a setback between them. He would run the risk. Her safety depended upon it.

Willa sighed and closed her eyes. Her breathing had grown even and regular. He began to dress. Annie could wake her later, after he was gone.

He was pulling on boots when Willa said, "Where are you going?" She wasn't asleep. He could have cursed. She sat up.

"Downstairs. I have something to discuss with Marshall." He pulled on his jacket.

Willa rose, her wet braid hanging down her back. "No, you haven't. You are going to find Ross. Matt, please—"

He kissed her objection away, and he kissed her the way he'd wanted to. He couldn't help himself. Their lips melded together. He brought a hand up to the tender skin right beneath her jawline, and he let his kiss tell her what he did not have time for words to say. He wanted her to stay here, waiting for him. Meanwhile, he was going to do everything he could to protect her.

Matt broke the kiss. Her eyes were dark and sensual. Her lips tried to follow him as he pulled away. "I think we are ready for each other, Willa. Be here when I return."

Then, before she could stop him, he walked swiftly out of the room, setting off for the Blue Boar.

Chapter 14

*H*er husband was a fool if he thought Willa would allow him to go after Ross and the dangerous Hardesty alone. He needed her.

She ran to the wardrobe. She grabbed the first day dress she saw, a marine blue with yellow lace, and threw it over her head, right over her nightgown.

Annie knocked and came into the room. "His Grace told me to see that you are put to bed—*what are you doing?*"

"I'm going after him," Willa said, pulling up socks. She sat on the floor in front of the wardrobe. "He is not going to leave me behind. Not if he thinks to go alone." She reached for her walking shoes, her fingers flying over the lacing.

"Your Grace, he does not want you to go. He told me to keep you here."

Willa came to her feet, straightening her skirts. "And how will you stop me?" she challenged. "If you come between me and my husband, Annie, don't doubt what my choice will be."

She tugged on a pelisse against the coolness of the day and then went over to the glass to do something with her hair.

"He is the *duke*," Annie worried. "The master of the house. If he thinks it best that you stay here, you should."

But Willa wasn't attending to a thing Annie said. Instead, she frowned at her reflection. She didn't have time to fidget with her hair. Matt certainly wasn't going to wait. She grabbed her sewing basket by a chair in the corner. She pulled out scissors. Without looking at the mirror, Willa began cutting at her braid.

Annie screamed her horror. Willa didn't care. She hacked with the scissors until Annie had the good sense to help. The braid was half gone by that point. Annie made quick work of the rest. She held the braid as if it was a weasel she had just killed.

Willa's head felt as if it could float off her shoulders. She ran a hand through her hair. It curved around her fingers in lovely curls.

"Who would have thought, Your Grace?" Annie said with a tone of wonder.

"It is nice, isn't it?"

"Better than I feared. But it needs to be evened."

"I don't have time. I'll wear a hat." She chose a burgundy velvet cap and set it at an angle on her head. "Don't try to stop me and don't tell on me, Annie. I'm trusting you." Willa walked to the door.

"Your husband will roast me alive."

Willa opened the door. "Nonsense. He'll be too busy fuming at me." She pressed her finger to her lips as an additional plea for Annie's trust, and then went out the door.

She started for the front steps but then thought differently. Matt would stop her if he could. The other servants owed their loyalty to him, not her. She could find herself locked in a closet.

Instead, she practically hurried down the back stairs. On the ground floor, she cracked open the stairway door and had a moment of confusion as she wondered which way to go next, toward the front door or out the back—then she heard Matt's deep voice in the foyer. He was still here.

There was a sound of a chair being pushed back in the breakfast room to Willa's right. She stepped back just in time to avoid being seen by the dowager as she exited the room. Minerva called to Matt as if just seeing him leave.

"Where are you off to?" his grandmother asked.

He answered something noncommittal. His words didn't carry

the way the dowager's did, but Willa could tell by his voice that he was impatient to go, *and* that he didn't want anyone to know what he was about.

With the duchess down the hall, Willa slid out the door and quietly moved to the rear of the house and out the very door Ross and Donel had carried her through only hours before. She moved to the front of the house, ducking behind a low wall when she saw Matt striding down the street.

Willa made up for her shorter legs with determination. She reached the street and started following Matt. He was on a mission. He walked to the end of the block to where there was more passing traffic.

She caught sight of what she should have noticed earlier. One of the footmen had been sent ahead of Matt and had hailed a hack. If she didn't hurry, he'd leave without her, and she was not going to let that happen.

"Toomey Street," Matt told the hack driver.

The man raised his brows as if to say that nothing good went on at Toomey Street. Matt could agree with him. However, once he handed the man coin, the driver was ready to go.

Matt climbed in. To reach their destination, the driver needed to travel in the opposite direction. He started to turn the corner but several young maids with shopping packages crossed the street in front of them. Matt settled back, annoyed at the delay—

The hack's door opened, and a petite woman climbed in and plopped herself right next to Matt. She had to lean out to the close the door.

"All right," Willa said. "I'm ready to go."

As if on command, the hack started on its way before Matt prodded himself to say, "You are not going." He leaned toward the window, ready to demand that the driver pull over, but Willa tugged him back.

"No, Matt, I am going. You can take me back to the house, but I will find another way to reach the Blue Boar."

"Willa, it is no place for a gentlewoman."

"I know. There is a murderer under its roof."

"Exactly. I can't let you risk your life."

She frowned as if he spoke gibberish. "I can't let you risk *your* life. I'm trying to protect you."

"Willa—"

"*Matt.*" Her voice overrode his. She was petite and ferocious. "I will not let you do this alone. I know it is dangerous. So was being bound and gagged and thrown in a river, but we managed— *together*—to escape. You need me, do you understand? And I need you. If something happens to you, well, I would never forgive myself. You can appreciate that, can't you? Would you let me go alone?"

"I don't want you to go at all—"

"I wonder if Kate would agree? Or Alice or Jenny or Amanda? Would you be so cruel as to leave me to face their wrath if they heard that I wasn't by your side when Hardesty did his worst?"

He started to protest again, and then realized it was useless. She perched on the seat beside him, her expressive eyes afire with sheer grit. She would find a way to follow him, a way that might be more dangerous than just accompanying him into the hellhole.

Besides, it was morning. The Blue Boar was a devil's stew in the darkness of night, but he doubted the rakes and thieves who were its usual custom were up and out this early.

And then he noticed a change about her. "What did you do to your hair?"

"Do you not like it?" she asked, giving her head a happy shake. "I believe it the best thing ever."

It was. Then again, his chipper, pushy, startlingly devoted wife could have shaved her head bald and he would have thought it the best thing ever. The curls actually made her appear to have more energy.

"Come here," he ordered. He touched her hair. It was soft and shining. How had he believed he'd ever loved Letty? She was a great beauty. But she lacked Willa's charm, her intelligence, her loyalty. With Willa, he was more himself. The light illuminating her was an inner one.

Willa took his arm and put it around her shoulders. She stifled a yawn. "Besides," she said, "you will keep me safe."

Had anyone ever trusted him so completely?

And secretly? He didn't mind having her with him on this trip to confront Ross and learn Hardesty's secrets. He was learning that often her thinking was clearer than his.

He put his other arm around her as well and pressed a kiss on the top of her velvet cap.

"I can't believe I cut it," Willa confessed.

"I can believe you will do anything," he answered. His response pleased her and she settled back in his arms.

They must have dozed, waking when the hack slowed to a stop.

Willa peered out the window. "I don't know where we are."

"Close to the docks," he answered. He climbed past her to open the door. Toomey Street was relatively normal at this time of the day. At the end of the road, the street was busy with merchants and sailors, the usual bustle going on. The fusty smell of wet rope blended with that of rotting fish and cooking foods. And underlying all was the Thames—which had its own unique smell.

He had no doubt that the Blue Boar was open. Whorehouses, especially in this area, rarely closed.

Matt paid the driver and helped Willa out. She looked around. "I don't find this threatening."

He didn't comment but put his arm around her waist, the way men and women commonly walked around this area.

They hadn't gone far before Willa whispered, "I rather like this. Are you treating me like a doxy?" He almost fell over his feet at the use of the word. Of course, she noticed and she laughed, the musical sound lighthearted.

"You are having too much fun with this," Matt accused.

"It is nice to go wherever I wish," she admitted, "provided I have a strong man beside me."

He liked the description.

But in the next breath, she asked, "Do you have an inkling where the Blue Boar is?"

"A bit," Matt answered. He nodded to a faded sign. One of the hinges was broken and all the metal was rusted with age and London's bad air. Time had weathered the blue boar's head, but the tusks could still be seen easily.

"Oh, dear," Willa said.

He opened the door. She drew a deep breath and marched through it.

The ground floor was blocked off and there were no stairs up. Instead, customers had to go downstairs to the tavern and a doorway that could be easily controlled. "Stay behind me," Matt ordered. He went down and opened a heavy door into a large tavern room that at night was packed with cardplayers and drinkers. There were several taps, and tables and chairs from one wall to the next.

This morning, the place appeared almost deserted. The air smelled of stale ale, old gin, and the odors of unwashed men. A group sat hunched over drinks and their cards. They appeared exhausted and gave Matt only a passing glance as he entered the room—until they saw Willa.

Then all heads turned. She was wise enough to wrap her arms around him. He was beginning to like her "doxy" role.

He walked up to the barman, a burly man with a grizzled growth of hair on his face and a belly as big as a sow's. Off to the side was a thin, yellow-haired woman. She had a hard face with a sharp nose. Her features weren't unattractive until one noticed the apron around her waist was filthy. She gave Matt a hard look over when he approached and then licked her lips.

Matt wasn't interested in an invitation. He set a coin in front of the man. "I'm looking for an Irishman named Ross."

"I'm not one for knowing Irishmen," the barman answered, his own brogue quite pronounced. He didn't make a move toward the coin.

However, the woman snatched it up. "I might be." She looked around the room and shrugged as if there wasn't anyone she feared present. "How do you know this Ross?"

"He has a horse for sale."

She nodded as if he'd confirmed a piece of information. "He can't pay what he owes me until he sells that damn nag."

"Where is he?"

She grinned. Her teeth were crooked and brown, and he knew what she waited for. He put another coin out. She answered, "He is upstairs with the other man who was asking after him."

"Another man?" Could it be Hardesty?

"Aye. It is a popular horse. Four legs and some hair. I don't understand." She nodded toward the back of the main room. There was another set of stairs with a door that he'd wager led to a hallway of doors. "You'll find Ross up there."

"Which room?"

"The first on the right," she said, confirming his suspicions. "If you wait for me, I'm the first room on the left."

"I just need Ross."

The men at the gaming table were now openly watching, their expressions assessing. Matt put his arm around Willa and started for the stairs.

"It will cost you if you pork that girl under my roof," the woman called.

Matt ignored her.

"She won't be as much fun as I am," the woman called. That earned comment from the cardplayers.

"Aye, Sally is a good one."

"So you say, Sal."

"I'd take what he has on his arm already." This was said by a greasy-haired character of indeterminate age.

"Well, they'd best keep quiet. You know my girls don't like to have their beauty sleep disturbed this time of the morning."

Everyone cackled at that.

Willa inched closer to Matt. "Why is it women are always offering themselves to you?" She sounded cranky. "And what did she mean by saying 'pork'?" Willa asked.

Matt grinned. "Treating you like my wife."

"Like your wife—? Oh."

The stairs were rickety. Matt felt them shake with every step. However, if Ross could walk up them, he was certain he could.

"Did you find that woman attractive?" Willa asked.

Matt stopped. "What woman?"

"The one down there."

"Willa, of course not." He opened the door and was relieved when he could finally close it behind them.

There was a short, narrow hallway with four doors to either side and a window on the far end. Blinding sunshine bounced off the dirty panes of glass. All was very quiet as if the occupants were sleeping after a hard night's work. There certainly wasn't the sound of two men talking. Could Hardesty have left already and the barmaid not told him? She had appeared perverse enough to be humored by such a trick.

Matt wasn't certain that Willa understood completely where they were, and he wanted to keep it that way.

Before looking for Ross's room, Matt walked to the window, wanting to know where he was. The window faced the wall of another building. There was a narrow space of perhaps a foot between the two buildings.

He started to turn, ready to take on Ross, when he heard a smart rap on Ross's door. Willa had taken it upon herself to knock. He hurried to her. "Could you wait for me? And why bother knocking?"

"I was being polite." There was a clip to her tone.

Matt frowned. "Are you angry?"

"No, why should I be?" More clipped tones. She stared at the door as if she could bore a hole through it with her eyes; her chin was set at that angle women adopted when they were spitting mad.

"You *are* angry."

She didn't bother to answer, but knocked again.

Matt leaned against the door frame, puzzled. "I have sisters. I know when women are angry with me."

Willa faced him. "I'm *tired* of your sisters. 'I have sisters,' " she mimicked. "I am not one of them. I have my *own* emotions."

"Such as jealousy?" The thought rather pleased him. It meant she cared.

She rounded on him as if he'd pinched her. Her chin lifted. "I'm not jealous. However, I'm tired of women always making over you. They are bothersome. No, worse, they are rude."

"You don't need to be jealous. Especially over that creature downstairs." He paused and added, "Or any other woman, Willa. Those lads were making comments about you."

"Apparently it didn't bother you."

"You were with me, and I know you have better taste than what they could offer."

"You are always so sure about things."

He frowned at her. "Do I need to be worried?" What was she saying?

Her glance met his eye and then shifted away. "We aren't a love match."

He might argue that point but before he could, she said, "Or truly man and wife."

Matt forgot about Ross and Hardesty and everything else in the world. "Are you telling me you are ready?"

"For you to *pork* me?"

Her use of the word made him grin. She was both bold and innocent. A fascinating combination.

"Yes, I am," she admitted, without waiting for his response. "I've thought about our conversation yesterday."

"And about last night?"

Her brows came together. "I want to trust you."

"You can—"

The door across the hall cracked open. "Pipe it down out there," a woman croaked out at them. The door slammed shut.

Willa gaped at the door that had opened, speculation in her eye.

"They sleep during the day," Matt explained.

"That really was a whore?" Her eyes widened as if she was scandalized but then she laughed, covering her mouth at the last minute to stifle the sound.

"I'm also done waiting for Ross," Matt said. He reached for the door handle. It wasn't locked. He pushed it open, ready to charge into the room—but then drew back immediately.

He thought to cover Willa's eyes, but he was too late. She was right behind him and had a good look at the Irishman in the bed, his throat cut and the sheets stained with blood. On the floor beside the bed was the body of a woman.

Willa's scream would have woken the dead.

Certainly, it woke the whores.

Chapter 15

The door across the hall opened. The strumpet marched furiously out of her room, her fists clenched. She wore a filthy chemise and nothing more. But she wasn't the only one. Sleepy, grumpy women in different stages of undress opened their doors to complain.

"I told you to pipe it down," the strumpet said, ready to take on Willa, until she caught a glimpse of Ross in the blood-soaked bed.

Her screams did not stop. She backed toward her doorway. The others surged forward and then began screaming and screaming.

Matt heard booted footsteps charging up the rickety staircase and he made a quick decision. Too many would jump to the wrong conclusion. He'd come looking for Ross and here Ross was dead. This was not a place where people listened to rational explanations.

"Come," he ordered, grabbing Willa's arm and running to the window. He tried to raise the sash. It wouldn't budge. He gave it another hard lift and it went up just as the door on the other end of the hall opened. The cardplayers came pouring in to mix with the screaming whores.

Matt lifted Willa through the window and said, "Run."

She ran, with him at her heels.

The space between the two buildings was a tight fit for him, but the sight of a man sticking his head out of the Blue Boar put wings to his feet.

They reached the street. Someone was coming out of the gaming den's front door. Matt took Willa's hand and they ran in the opposite direction. She was breathing heavily, but she was a game one. She did not give up.

Matt dragged her into one of the pubs, racing with her to the back of the establishment. He found a back door and dashed out into the alley.

This section of London was a maze of side streets and alleyways. He kept them moving until they reached a busy thoroughfare. Bermondsey. He sighed his relief. The traffic was heavier.

"Are you all right?" he asked Willa. She'd lost her saucy velvet cap. He had no idea where his hat had fallen off, either.

"There was so much blood," she said. "And his throat—"

He nodded and tucked her hand in the crook of his arm. "Let's just walk. We are all right. No one should associate us with that."

"So much blood."

"Willa, don't think on it."

"How can I not? There was another body in the room, wasn't there? How could Hardesty kill both of them?"

"He didn't want a witness."

"That poor girl."

Matt nodded, his attention taken by the sight of a hack making its way down the street. He waved, catching the driver's attention. He gave the driver his address and climbed into the cab after Willa.

She all but collapsed in his arms. They held each other close. His heart still pounded from the escape. She had her head against his chest and gripped a portion of his shirt.

It was a great relief to see the hack turning onto London Bridge.

"Matt, what is going on?"

"I'm not certain," he answered.

"But you have a suspicion? You asked after Hardesty."

"I'd hoped he was with Ross."

"Apparently, he was." She lifted her head. "But the woman didn't say anything about him leaving. He could have been there and we wouldn't have known because we don't know who he is." She paused, her gaze arrowing on him. "Unless you believe you know this Hardesty. Do you?"

He looked down at her, his courageous, wild, little wren. "The less you know, the better."

"Obviously not," she reminded him. "Is Hardesty someone close to you? That you have met? That I could know?"

"Willa, if what I believe is true, then this could upend my family. Until I'm certain, silence is your protection."

She pushed away from him, sitting up.

"Willa—"

"No, Matt, I will not be placated."

"That isn't it at all."

"It isn't? This does concern me. And I'm tired of being 'protected.' Even if there hadn't been an attempt on my life, I'd be concerned because Hardesty is apparently determined to see you dead. I'm not ready to let go of you yet. Or perhaps I'm not the woman you want." She sat back on the seat, keeping a distance from him. "I hadn't thought of it that way."

"Willa, you are misinterpreting—"

The hack pulled up in front of the house. Instead of staying so they could talk, Willa opened the door and hopped right out. She strode into the house, where Marshall held open the door. Her movement was purposeful, her displeasure clear. Matt had to pay the driver before he could follow her as quickly as possible.

By the time he entered the house, she had already gone upstairs. She might be petite, but she could move fast.

"Excuse me, Your Grace," Marshall said, approaching him. "The dowager is out; however, she instructed me to remind you of the Mallory dinner party this evening."

"The Mallory dinner party?"

"Sir Bernard and Dame Sarah Mallory are hosting a dinner in honor of a visiting Italian singer."

After what Matt had been through over the last evening and morning, there was no possible way that he was going to listen to

Italian warbling while dancing attendance on his grandmother. "Tell her my wife and I must beg off. We desire this evening for ourselves." Minerva would be annoyed, but Matt had other plans and they all centered on Willa. He took the stairs two at a time.

Their bedroom door was open. The bath had been cleaned up by the ever-efficient Annie. Willa was pulling stacks of clothes out of the wardrobe.

"What are you doing?" he asked from the doorway.

"I'm moving. I no longer wish to share a bedroom with you." She began pulling out shoes. One of them was his. She threw it back into the wardrobe.

"We aren't going to have separate bedrooms," Matt said.

She looked up at him. "You don't make all the rules, Your Grace."

"My house."

"My money."

He didn't like that comment. "What am I going to do? Pork you from afar?"

She had no answer. He decided to ask a question that would grab her attention. "Are you truly in love with me?"

That stopped her movements. She didn't look at him.

Matt closed the door. "You told me you were."

"I don't remember saying that," Willa said slowly.

"It was last night when you were angry with me over Letty."

"When I felt *betrayed* finding you with Lady Bainhurst."

He didn't answer.

She folded the piece of clothing she held in her hand and then offered, "You have been kind to me. Kinder than I believe most husbands would be."

"That isn't what I'm asking, Willa. Do you love me?"

Willa rose to her feet. "If love means that I worry if you are danger? Yes. If it means that I want to be a helpmate to you, to be a partner in all things, then yes. If it means that I want to trust you, but wonder if you have a care for me, well, yes."

"And when did you decide you were in love with me?"

"I don't know." Willa put her hand on the bedpost. "It wasn't this burst of understanding like fireworks. Or my heart pounding in my chest every time I looked at you . . . although I do like to look at you, Matt—especially when you are sleeping. Your guard is down then."

She was right.

"In truth," Willa continued, "I often find you exasperating because you don't always do what I expect."

"I can appreciate the feeling."

That comment caught her attention. He held out his hands as if to declare his innocence. "You jilted me, Willa. With a snap of your fingers."

A light came to her eyes. "I did, didn't I?"

"It woke me up." He took a step toward her. "Everything you do makes me more aware of what I'm saying and how I'm acting."

Willa nodded. "Yes, like that. I understand. Love is quieter than I thought it would be, Matt. I read your poems—no, don't scoff. They are lovely."

"Willa—"

"They are meaningful to me," she revised, "because they say something about you. And I admire how you are kind to people. No arrogance. No airs."

"Thank you."

Her lips twisted in self-deprecation before she said, "And then you married me even though you didn't truly want me. But you have been thoughtful and giving."

"Willa, I want you."

She shook her head as if to deny him. She crossed over to the desk and sat in the chair. She looked out the window, and he could feel a chasm forming between them. She was right; in protecting her, he was shutting her out.

He wouldn't have liked that, either.

Matt spoke. "I believe my cousin George is Hardesty."

Her expressive eyes widening, she faced him. "The lawyer?"

Matt nodded.

She frowned. "I have trouble connecting the fastidious George with the blood in Ross's room."

"I know, and yet, Hardesty knows things that only someone in the family would know."

"What possible reason could he have? He is a successful man. Even my father admires him."

"The oldest in the world—jealousy." He walked over to the desk and sat in the chair opposite hers, eager to share his theory. "George's father and my grandfather were twins. It has always been a bit of a family jest that George's father should have been quicker. Well, it was a jest for Henry. George seemed good-humored."

"But if he wasn't?"

He leaned on the desk. "Exactly. George has been kind to me, but in ways that my grandparents would have disapproved."

"For example?"

"He came to my father's funeral when Henry had declared no one should attend. He defied Henry, but not in an overt way. And to be honest, Henry probably didn't care. He used George's services, but I never heard him give the man any consideration."

"But could George slit Ross's throat?"

"Could he hire men to kill us? Grandmother is convinced Hardesty had a hand in William's riding accident."

Willa chewed on the thought a moment. "George hired men for you to catch Hardesty."

"He did for Grandfather as well."

"Have you met these men?"

Matt drew a deep breath. "I'm wondering if I have. If Ross and Donel were the men he hired."

"So he blackmailed the old duke just for money?" Matt understood that sort of greed was beyond Willa's understanding. Her father would have grasped it immediately.

"Or to balance matters out," he said. "Perhaps he felt he deserved Camberly. He did know about William. He told me so."

"My mother mentioned William last night. She was aware of his nature. Apparently, it wasn't that big of a secret."

"Neither was my infatuation with Letty Bainhurst. However, the stationery used for the notes sent to both Letty and me was from a study in the Evanston house. George was there. He had the opportunity to arrange everything."

"Including telling Lady Evanston that you wished to see me when you were with Letty. I did notice George in the card room."

"I saw him as well. He appeared to be playing but perhaps he was watching."

"How would he know that I'd be angry and leave? Why would he wish to drive a wedge between us?"

"I don't know, but I will ask him when I see him."

"We must go to the magistrate."

"We can't prove any of this, Willa. I could even be wrong and performing a terrible injustice to George. For that reason, I will handle the matter myself."

"Matt, no—"

"It's my family, Willa. My responsibility. The last thing the title needs is more of our personal affairs airing out in public."

"If George is a murderer, there is no way this will be kept quiet. Nor can you let him go. We'll always be looking over our shoulders."

She was right.

Matt stood. "Come here."

Willa looked uncertain. She came to her feet and walked over to him.

Almost reverently, he bent down, seeking her lips. "I'm fortunate to be married to a wise woman," he whispered, his mouth inches from hers.

"I pray you never forget that statement," she whispered back, and then he kissed her.

He kissed her reverently, hopefully, passionately.

Her arms came around his neck. She stood on her toes. He picked her up and carried her to the bed. His fingers began working her lacings. Her hands slid inside his jacket, pushing it down over his shoulders.

Dear God, he wanted this. He'd had her warmth beside him in bed but it had taken all his willpower to give her the time she needed to heal.

Matt lowered his arms, and his jacket slid to the floor. He pulled Willa down onto the bed beside him. He kissed her chin, her cheek, her nose, and her sweet ears before finding her mouth again. She laughed as if it tickled, and the sound made his heart grow fuller, the beat stronger.

She loved him.

He'd always thought true love was full of drama and turmoil. It wasn't. Love was the sense that he was right where he was supposed to be. That at last, he'd found his home.

They undressed in earnest now. Clothes were thrown, boots tugged off, ribbons unbound. He buried his hands in her hair, adoring the silky texture of her curls. He liked her hair. He'd tell her that . . . as soon as he finished letting her know how much he loved her . . .

That was Matt's last thought. They were between the cool cotton sheets. The mattress felt good and having Willa beside him felt even better. This was the best of married life and he couldn't wait to be inside his wife.

"Are you ready to count?" he teased, reminding her of her mother's advice to count backward and it would all be done.

Willa laughed against his lips, her breasts flattened against his chest, her hips fitting with his. With one hand, he cupped her buttocks to him. "One hundred," he said.

"Ninety-nine," she answered.

"Ninety-eight." He nipped her shoulder and then found her mouth and swallowed her "Ninety-seven."

The tip of his shaft was right there. He pressed forward, sliding it between her legs, knowing how sensitive she was.

She opened herself to him. "Ninety-six."

Matt looked down at her. "Willa, don't ever be jealous again. You are the only woman I want."

Her response was to shift beneath him, positioning right where he wanted to be.

"The only one," she echoed.

"Forever," he promised.

She smiled. No one had a smile like Willa's. It lit his heart, until it turned slyly wicked.

"So, are you going to 'pork' that lady, sir?" Her imitation of the Blue Boar's strumpet was so spot-on, he couldn't help but laugh. "Or are you just going to tease her until she goes mad?"

His response was to thrust forward.

This time there was no barrier. She was snug around him. He held himself, watching her. "Is it all right?"

She wiggled her hips as if sampling the position and then ran her hand down his side. "It's perfect. Is this it?"

"This is only the beginning." And it was.

The very heat of her took hold of him. He began to move with purpose. Willa was as responsive as he had thought she would be. At first, he tried to hold back, but she wouldn't let him. She moved with an urgency of her own—and then she cried out his name.

His first reaction was that he'd harmed her.

He started to pull out, but her arms wrapped around his. "No, Matt, no. Please, no." She pressed herself against him. He pushed deeper, and her whimper wasn't from pain, but pleasure.

His little Willa was a noisy lover, and the sounds of her gasps and coos drove him into a fine madness. He could not do enough to please her.

The tension between them built, fine-tuning itself until that moment when everything peaked.

Deep muscles held him; her beautiful, supple body arched against him. Wave after wave of rippling roiled through her.

And Matt came with her. Life flowed between them.

When they were done and spent, she nestled her head against his chest and they fell into a peaceful sleep.

WILLA WOKE FIRST.

Her head rested on the same pillow as the one Matt was using. For a second, she breathed in the scent of him. His skin was warm beneath her palm.

She loved him so much, she could not imagine the world without him. *You are the only woman I want.* His words were magic to her.

His eyes opened. He rolled on his back and stretched. The mattress moved beneath her and she laughed.

At the sound, Matt whipped his head in her direction. He smiled. "Good morning."

"Good evening," she countered.

He frowned as if remembering. "What time is it?"

She shook her head.

Matt sat up and put his feet over the side of the bed. He combed his hair before rising and walking over to the washbasin where there was a fob watch.

"It is almost eight," he said. "I need to eat."

Willa's stomach rumbled her reply. He laughed and poured water into the basin. "I'm certain they are waiting supper for us," he said. He picked up the dress Willa had been wearing and tossed it to her before washing.

She ran a hand over her curls. She was glad she'd cut her hair. Sleeping had been easier, and considering how much moving around she and Matt had done when they made love, well, that was easier as well. She nudged Matt out of the way of the washbasin so she could see her hair in the glass.

"I adore it," she said. She looked at her husband. "What do you think?"

"I think I adore you."

Willa grinned and began her toilette.

Within the half hour, they were on their way downstairs to the dining room.

Marshall met them at the foot of the stairs. "We are hungry," Matt said to the butler.

"Cook has kept supper warm. I shall order it be served."

"Please tell her to keep it simple," Matt said. "We will eat in the sitting room." That was where they usually sipped their port and sherry.

"Yes, Your Grace."

"Also, has my grandmother eaten?" Matt looked to Willa. "She wanted us to accompany her to a dinner party this evening, but I knew we would be exhausted. I told her we couldn't."

"Thank you," Willa said.

"Yes, well, she may not be pleased with us."

"The dowager is not here, Your Grace. She did go to Sir Bernard's affair."

"Did she go by herself?"

"No, Your Grace. Mr. Addison went with her."

Matt went still. He looked to Willa, who shared his worry. "When should she return?" Willa asked.

"She said it could be a late evening. She is fond of Sir Bernard and his wife. Also, Mr. Addison left this note for you."

The paper was the same one that had been used at the ball.

The seal was unmarked. Matt broke it. He leaned toward Willa so that she could see the message as well: *Meet me at Mayfield.*

There was no signature, but then one wasn't needed.

George knew Matt was onto his game.

"We must go to the magistrate," Willa said.

The smile Matt gave her was cold. "If he does anything to her, I will break his neck."

Willa understood. "I don't believe that is his plan. His actions are desperate. He knows it is over."

Matt frowned. "It is going to be over."

She took charge. "Marshall, saddle two horses immediately."

She started for the door. "I shall be down in two shakes, Your Grace. I must change into my riding habit."

"Willa, I want you to stay here—"

She turned on him, holding up a hand to stop his words. "Have you learned nothing this day? You need me."

On those words, she dashed up the stairs to change into her smart military-styled habit.

And to her relief, he waited for her to come down.

Chapter 16

Within the hour, they had eaten a light meal and were ready for the ride ahead. Matt had taken time to write several important letters and send servants to deliver them. One was to the magistrate in Essex. Another to the sheriff. Two more were to neighbors. Whatever George had planned, Matt was not going to let him escape justice.

Furthermore, his wife was right. This was a legal matter. Witnesses were needed. He invited all parties to meet him with due haste at Mayfield.

He and Willa set out.

Matt found himself on a hired gelding. Willa rode the unruly mare, who was a jewel for her. Either that, or Willa sat a better seat than Matt did.

Even though it was a half moon, they followed a main road and had little difficulty. They didn't talk. They were riding too hard. Matt was grateful for Willa's presence.

He tried not to think about what could happen to his grandmother. He carried a loaded pistol in his pocket and a knife in his boot. God willing, he'd not have to use either.

They reached Mayfield shortly before midnight. Once in sight of the house, Matt reined in.

When he was in London, the country house had a small staff of locals who often went home for the evenings. The retainers, such as Marshall and Mrs. Snow and Cook, journeyed back and forth but spent the bulk of their time in the city.

Right now, Mayfield looked deserted. Its brick walls reflected what little moonlight there was. No lights shone from the window. Not even a dog barked since the dogs would have been put up for the night down by the stables.

"I want you to stay here and wait for the magistrate or anyone else who might come," he instructed Willa.

"Why don't you wait as well?"

"I have to go there."

"Matt, he might not be there."

"He's there." He started to ride away and then turned his horse around. He went back to his wife. Bringing his horse up alongside hers, he pulled Willa to him and kissed her long and hard on the mouth.

"Take care," she whispered when they were done.

"I will. I have too much to live for." He placed a gloved hand against the side of her face. It would be so tempting to wait. To be safe. And yet, it was up to him to bring George to heel.

He also feared what would happen to Minerva if George thought Matt was not alone.

"Wait," he commanded Willa one last time.

She nodded dutifully.

He whirled his horse around and rode up the drive to his front door. He dismounted and tied his horse to a post by the front door. He walked to the door. It was slightly ajar.

Matt pushed it open. The hinges didn't even creak. He moved into the hall, and then stopped at the sight he saw in the front sitting room.

In a patch of moonlight from the window Minerva sat bound and gagged in a chair. Her hair fell to her shoulders and she was pale and shaking.

Taking out the pistol, Matt said quietly, "I'm here, Grandmother."

She nodded her head and tried to make sounds. Matt didn't

understand until he heard a footfall behind him and then the heaviness of George's breathing.

Matt dodged just in time to avoid being cleaved in two by the axe George was wielding. His hand holding the pistol hit the doorjamb. Matt lost control of the weapon. It went flying into the shadows.

Meanwhile, George had fallen forward from the force of his swing, but he quickly regained his footing. He jumped at Matt, the axe high in his hands. In shadows and moonlight, with his hair going every which way, George appeared demented. He grinned. "Well, this appears to be it."

"What is 'it,' George?" Matt tried to keep his voice steady.

"Everything. It is all lost now, Matt." With a wild grunt, he lunged at Matt with the axe, swinging it with both hands.

Matt jumped back. The axe just barely missed him. He thought of the knife in his boot. It was no match for an axe. He needed the pistol. He took a step in the direction he thought it had fallen.

"George, you need to stop this. The magistrate is coming. It will be worse for you if anything happens to Minerva or me."

"The worst has already happened," George answered. His shoulders sagged. He stood between Matt and the door. But it didn't make any difference, Matt would not leave Minerva behind. "I won't make it out of this," George predicted.

"No, you won't," Matt agreed. In the chair, Minerva was weeping. "You'll not make it, either."

Matt was determined that he was going to be wrong about that. But he wanted to keep George talking. He wanted answers. "Because you want the title for your sons." George had three of them. The oldest was James.

"Am I that obvious?" George swung the axe viciously. Again, Matt managed to avoid the deadly blade, but it was becoming more difficult. George was pushing toward the corner of the room. "After all, *I'm* done. I'll hang for my deeds, but my descendants will be Camberly."

"It didn't start off that way, did it? In the beginning, all you wanted was the money."

"Because it could have been mine," George answered. "My father and Henry were twins. It could have gone either way. And then I had to watch the old bastard squander what had been given to him. Henry chased every silly notion that crossed his head. I'd advise him not to do it. He never listened to me."

"Therefore, you took his money."

"You aren't listening, Your Grace. It should have been mine."

"And the murders? Did you have a hand in William's death?"

"No. The silly sod killed himself. Always riding animals too spirited for him—" He swung the axe as if he believed he had lulled Matt into complacency.

He hadn't. However, the action did force Matt two more steps toward the corner.

"What of Ross and that woman this morning?"

George shot Matt a look of pure reproach. "What of Donel? Your hands aren't clean, Your Grace." He pointed the axe at Matt in triumph. "You didn't think I suspected what happened."

"I had little choice in the matter, cuz. It was him or me."

"The same with Ross. When I found out that he'd let you escape because he wanted to sell a horse . . . well, I lost my temper. I also knew it was over for me. You would reason it out."

"Why do you want to kill me?"

"Because I must. You see, William and Henry's deaths were unfortunate but natural. And then, there you were. Unsuited for the role of Camberly. You didn't have an idea about anything. And I knew so much. I could have made this into a great estate."

"It would have been a great deal better off if you hadn't robbed my grandfather blind."

"He could have refused to pay," George said reasonably.

"Then he would be exposing William."

George shrugged. "His choice."

"So you wish to kill me because I'm not a good duke?" Matt pressed.

"No, I wanted to kill you because I realized, I could have it all." George gifted him with another mighty swing of his axe. It hit a side table, destroying it, and pushed Matt farther into the corner. "And now James will have it. My precious son."

His voice had taken on a sing-song. He was obviously in a bad state. All Matt needed was a second's inattention.

"What is the plan?" Matt asked. "You kill me and then what happens to my grandmother?"

"She dies as well. We all die, right here in this house. I'll take my own life and pay for my sins. But first, I'll set the house on fire. Mayfield will be burned to the ground. There will be mourning, especially from your lovely wife." He sighed with regret. "But I won't let you escape this time. There is too much at stake."

"Do you believe Willa won't tell everyone how you tried to have us murdered in the river? What you have done might taint your son's chance to inherit the title."

"Not legally. After all, he didn't have a hand in my deeds. And people really aren't all that interested in you, Matt. They will hear about the fire and everyone will believe it was an accident—"

"Except me," a female voice said.

Willa stood in the door. Matt didn't know how long she'd been there. He would give her a royal scolding for disobeying his order to wait for the officers of the law.

However, she did provide the distraction Matt needed.

George jumped at the unexpected sound of her voice, and Matt charged. He hit George full-on with his body weight. Matt was younger and a bit taller, but George had the strength of madness.

They fell against Minerva in the chair, knocking her over. Both of them lost their balance. Matt grabbed George's coat, hanging on and trying to keep as close to him as he could.

George scrambled up. He held the axe with two hands. *"Let me go,"* he was shouting. *"Let me go or I kill her."* He was speaking of Minerva, who was on her side on the floor. He started to swing the axe.

Matt grabbed at his arm and threw him onto the ground, pinning George with his weight. Holding him down, Matt sat up and punched his cousin in the head—once, twice, and George was out, his nose bloodied.

Uncertain if George was bluffing, Matt stayed right where he was, ready to strike again—

"Your Grace?"

Matt looked up and was surprised to see the sitting room full of men carrying lamps.

And there was Willa, helping a gentleman lift Minerva, still tied to her chair, to a sitting position.

Matt started for Willa. He didn't know if he would give her a lecture on the danger of not listening to him or kiss her silly.

She looked up at him just then—and he knew he wanted to kiss her silly.

Someone untied Minerva and took the gag from her mouth. She burst into noisy tears and held her hands out for Matt. He helped her rise. She was very shaky and he understood why. The old girl had been through a great deal this evening. He himself was exhausted.

His grandmother put her arms around him and sobbed. Matt looked to Willa for guidance. "Hold her," she mouthed.

In all the time he had been around Minerva, she had never asked for affection, not even the simplest of hugs. He put his arms around her and felt her tension ease.

"He didn't kill William," she said between sobs for Matt's ears alone. "I could have sworn he had. It's as if I feel the pain of losing my son all over again. I can't believe William could have just fallen off. He could ride anything."

There it was, she focused on William and ignored her other son, his father. Or the danger they'd all just experienced.

And yet, Matt heard his father's calm voice when he said, "Perhaps George did have a hand in it, Grandmother. I'm certain William felt the weight of being the source of the blackmail."

"I'm certain he did."

Willa offered a kerchief, which Minerva gratefully accepted. "I believe you should rest," Willa suggested.

"I would like to rest," Minerva agreed. "This has been very hard. I didn't know George was taking me to Mayfield until we were on the road. It was as if he changed into another person. He even hit me and he said vile things. I never knew he felt that way."

"He hid it well," Matt answered.

On the floor, George started groaning as he returned to consciousness. Two men picked him up. Matt recognized them as his stable lads.

"I fetched them," Willa said proudly. "I was waiting as you told me to," she added hurriedly, "but I worried, and I thought you could use help."

"Why didn't they come in here instead of you? Willa, George could have murdered you."

"But you would have stopped him," she said with every confidence. "I knew I would be safe."

He kissed her then. He didn't care if they had an audience. Such trust must be rewarded.

A clearing of a throat brought Matt back to the present moment.

"Your Grace, I'm Lord Dumfries, the magistrate."

"Yes, I remember meeting you. Thank you for coming."

Dumfries was a slender fellow with blond graying hair. "I almost didn't. But your letter was such that I knew I must rouse myself from my bed to see if it was true."

"Are you disappointed?"

The magistrate looked around at the damage in the room. "I am not. However, will you tell us the story?"

"And is there a place we can lock this man up?" Squire Tarlton, who served as sheriff, asked. "I'll have men come and pick him up in the morning."

"Capital idea," Matt agreed. He directed the stable lads to see that George was locked up in the grain room.

George wasn't vocal. He looked around as if in a daze. He was probably stunned at how far he'd fallen, and how this would be his legacy to his children. Matt pitied the boys.

"Shall we go into the dining room?" Matt offered. "We can all sit around the table and hear the story out over a glass of whisky." Even Minerva thought that was a splendid idea.

Matt told the story. Willa sat beside him, silent—for once. Minerva shared her harrowing adventure of being kidnapped. The squire had asked for paper and ink and he recorded their versions of events.

The whisky helped the dowager recover. When Dumfries asked if Matt wished to take out charges against George, she answered, "Absolutely not."

"Grandmother, we will," Matt answered.

"We can't," she countered. "What will people think? We don't want our affairs to be bandied about."

"He killed people," Willa said. "I saw their bodies. What he did was terrible."

"Bodies?" Minerva echoed. "A dockside doxy and some man no one knows? They don't count for anything."

"The law frowns on murder, Your Grace," Dumfries said tactfully.

"I don't care what the law frowns on. The title must not be attached to any such sordid business."

"He tried to murder us—" Willa answered, starting to her feet in her indignation.

Matt reached out to place a hand on her shoulder. He looked to Dumfries. "Of course charges should be filed. And prepare yourself. My cousin is an excellent lawyer."

"*Your Grace,*" Minerva started. "I must object—"

"And you are free to do so, Grandmother. However, it is my decision that carries weight. I'm tired of secrets. I'm done with them. George will be judged for his actions."

"He will sully our name—"

"He already has," Matt said. "We should have talked to the authorities years ago."

She shut her mouth then. He knew she didn't agree with him. That was fine. He was Camberly.

It was almost dawn by the time everything was settled. The squire said, "I suppose it will be this afternoon when I send lads over."

"Whenever will be fine," Matt assured him. "My cousin is not going anywhere."

At last everyone was gone. Minerva had sought her bed over an hour earlier, obviously disheartened that she would not have her way.

Now it was just Matt and Willa. He held out his arms, and she walked directly into them.

Matt kissed the top of her head. She cozied closer. This charming, beautiful woman had been willing to risk her life for him. What's more, she loved him . . .

"I have a confession to make."

She yawned. "Can it wait for morning?"

"I fear not."

He had her complete attention now. "What is it? You look so serious."

"I am serious." He sat her down at the table and took the chair next to hers. Her feet barely touched the floor. Sometimes he felt twice her size. Right now, he believed he was a very little man. "I have a confession to make," he started. "My conscience won't let me go until I tell you the truth."

"Very well." She folded her hands in her lap.

Matt sat a moment, preparing himself before admitting, "I didn't choose or even purchase the marriage ring you wear. I hadn't done anything for the wedding, including asking a groomsman. I contacted Soren in the middle of the night demanding he fill the role."

"Why are you telling me this?"

"Because I wish to be worthy of you. I notice how often you touch the ring."

She curled her fingers in her lap. "It matches my tastes perfectly. I'm fond of it."

"And you thought I had chosen it."

Willa looked down at the ring and then slowly nodded her head.

Matt slid off his chair and came down on one knee. "I'm sorry that I didn't give you the respect you deserved." He placed his hand over hers. "But if you will forgive me, I'll work every day to make it up to you. I love you, Willa. Passionately, fully, and completely. There is no other woman who has ever touched my heart with her bravery and my soul with love. I give all I have to you, Willa. Everything. This is my solemn vow because I never want to lose you."

Tears welled in her eyes. He feared he had upset her. "Willa, have I said the wrong thing?"

"You have said all the right things," she answered—and then she threw her arms around him. "Of course I forgive you, but please let me hear you say it again."

"Ask you to forgive me?"

"No, you buffle-headed man. The part that is important."

He understood. "I love you, Willa. I'll always love you—"

She cut him off with a kiss. They took their time of it, enjoying the moment.

Matt rose from the ground, picking up his petite bride. She looked at him. "I have a confession as well."

"Yes."

"When I wrote the letter jilting you, I'd hoped that you would come for me, and you did. Now I am no longer a blank piece of paper."

"What do you mean?"

"The day I wrote the letter, I tried to make a list of all the things I wanted out of my life. I couldn't think of anything. I was too dull and lacked experience in life. You changed that, Matt. We've been kidnapped, and almost murdered, and visited a whorehouse."

"These aren't necessarily good things, Willa."

"But they proved that *together*, we can face anything. And now, take me to bed, husband. We have much catching up to do."

Matt was happy to oblige.

Epilogue

Cornwall
May 7, 1814

here were babies. Beautiful, healthy, plump babies.

And Willa had never seen her two friends happier. Motherhood suited Leonie and Cassandra.

As the three friends had promised themselves, they gathered with husbands and children at the first opportunity.

Leonie's daughter, Lady Elizabeth Rose Gilchrist, was almost nine months. She had her mother's exotic eyes and her father's smile. She was already attempting to walk.

"Precocious like her mother," Leonie's husband, Roman, Lord Rochdale, said proudly. Cassandra's son was two months and four days old. Lord Andrew Lawrence York had an awareness of his surroundings that surprised Willa for someone so young. His six-year-old half brother, Lord Logan, doted on him with gentle care. Willa was deeply touched to watch the two brothers together.

They were all at the Dewsberry estate, Pentreath Castle, because of Andrew's age.

After what seemed to be weeks of rain, they were enjoying a sunny day. The husbands, Logan, and Willa had all gone for a bit of fishing before joining the new mothers on the back portico. The talk was of building projects, land management, Leonie's roses for which she was becoming renowned, and the school that Cassandra and Soren had opened.

Willa sat in her chair on the back portico, where their hosts had prepared what could only be described as a feast, and listened to the happy sharing. The men were entertaining Logan by teaching him how to play croquet. Their voices carried across the lawn.

"There isn't a game Logan doesn't enjoy," Cassandra said with a touch of pride. "His mind is so quick."

"He will grow into quite a man," Willa agreed. She was holding Andrew and enjoying the soft, cottony smell of him.

Her friends had asked questions about the case against George. He was coming up for trial in a few weeks. The papers and pamphleteers were busy making him and his misdeeds infamous. Only Minerva was upset by the gossip and speculation. Willa and Matt were at peace with their decision.

Baby Andrew's head bobbled slightly as he looked up at her. She smiled down at him—and then he spit up.

"Oh, I'm so sorry," Cassandra said, jumping to her feet with a wet cloth to help Willa clean up.

"It's fine," Willa said, and it was. "He is being a baby." She handed Andrew to his mother and dabbed at the shoulder of her dress.

"I don't have an article of clothing that doesn't have some stain from Lizzy," Leonie said.

"It is time for him to nurse anyway," Cassandra answered. "We'll only be a moment." She slipped inside the house.

"I will have to do that shortly as well," Leonie said. "But this is our first private moment since we arrived." She leaned toward Willa. "You appear so happy. The marriage is good?"

Willa thought of that morning, of her husband's lovemaking. She ran a finger over the lines of her wedding ring, the one Matt had made perfect with his confession and vow of honesty. He'd kept that vow.

"My marriage is wonderful."

Leonie smiled. "We are three lucky women." Her gaze drifted

to the tall men in deep competition with themselves and a small boy. "Logan will outfox them."

"Undoubtedly."

"I didn't mention it earlier, but I do like your hair. The style suits you. It is as if you were weighed down before and now you seem lighter."

"That is how I feel."

"And children?" Leonie asked.

"In God's time," Willa said. "To be honest, right now, life is so full." A memory struck her. "Before Matt and I married, I tried to make a list of all the things I wanted to do in my life. I was lonely after you and Cassandra married and left. The pages were blank. I knew nothing, had thought of nothing. I'd spent all the time until that moment meeting others' expectations. I tried to be what my parents wanted."

"They wanted us to find husbands."

"And to not cause any comment or scandals," Willa added.

"True," Leonie agreed. "How is your father with all the gossip about the trial coming up?"

"He is too concerned with his own affairs to have a care. I'm not sorry we are doing this. People have taken Matt aside and told him stories of disgrace from their own families. It is almost as if they had carried a burden and must confess it to him." She looked over to her husband, who had knocked his wooden ball into Roman's and sent it flying. "I love him so deeply that I can't imagine my life without him."

"I understand. I never could have believed I would be this happy."

Willa swung around in her chair to face Leonie. "But it is more than having a husband. With Matt, I have someone who wishes me to be my best self. In turn, I want the same for him. The gossip and rumors about the trial are nothing to us as long as we have each other."

"And our friends," Leonie said. "As long as we are friends."

"I could second that," Willa answered.

"Second what?" Cassandra said, coming out onto the portico. She must have handed Andrew over to his nurse for a nap since he wasn't in her arms.

"Our friendship," Leonie said. "It has taken us through many adventures."

"Because we have been there to support each other," Cassandra answered. She poured a glass of lemonade. She offered it to Leonie and then poured two more.

"And to compete with each other," Willa reminded them. "I did win our point game."

"I am convinced we have all come out winners," Leonie answered.

"So, here is to friendship," Cassandra said, sitting down and raising her glass.

"And to the future," Willa offered.

"May we be women unafraid to face whatever life brings us," Leonie finished.

And it was so.

Author's Note

Dear Readers—

I come from a long line of strong women. We didn't set off to be "strong." Often, we didn't always know what we were about. We were merely meeting others' expectations. We just did the next right thing as it appeared before us. We made mistakes in life . . . and learned valuable lessons.

We lived fully.

Is it true we find ourselves through love? Or is it when we are open to love with its powers of healing and grace that we can find ourselves? I believe the answer is unique to each of us.

Things I do know—friendship is a saving grace. And finding a partner in life who helps me be all that I can is a true blessing.

Leonie, Cassandra, and Willa, the Spinster Heiresses, may not be perfect. However, through love, they keep seeking the very best in themselves. Each of us can ask no more.

And I've learned that love is more than just focusing on one person. There are many things to love in this life, such as the freedom to think for ourselves or to find joy in the passions and experiences that make life worth living. It is all about engagement.

Finally, a word about William. I wanted to write a black-mail book. My research led me to discover that there was really only one reason for blackmail during this time period, and that was homosexuality.

You see, scandal was an everyday occurrence. Women and men cheated on each other. Babies were born happily and un-happily out of wedlock. There was embezzlement and fraud, murder and mayhem, even a few bombings, and an assassination. The Regency was a colorful age.

But there was only one topic that could destroy a man, making him a ripe target for the blackmailer. Thankfully, we have moved beyond those prejudices. I hope I have treated William with respect.

And now, here are my wishes for you—may you love well, may you surround yourself with people who help you be your best self, and may you never stop living fully.

With much love,
Cathy Maxwell
Buda, Texas
June 1, 2018